Bluebeard

Bluebeard

A NOVEL BY

KURT VONNEGUT

DELACORTE PRESS/NEW YORK

Published by
Delacorte Press
1 Dag Hammarskjold Plaza
New York, New York 10017

Manufactured in the United States of America

First trade edition

Designed by Judith Neuman-Cantor

A signed first edition of this book has been privately printed by
The Franklin Library.

Library of Congress Cataloging in Publication Data

Vonnegut, Kurt.
  Bluebeard.

  I. Title.
PS3572.05B5   1987   813'.54   87–14677
ISBN 0-385-29590-1

AUTHOR'S NOTE:

This is a novel, and a hoax autobiography at that. It is not to be taken as a responsible history of the Abstract Expressionist school of painting, the first major art movement to originate in the United States of America. It is a history of nothing but my own idiosyncratic responses to this or that.

Rabo Karabekian never lived, and neither did Terry Kitchen or Circe Berman or Paul Slazinger or Dan Gregory or Edith Taft or Marilee Kemp or any of the other major characters in this book. As for real and famous persons I mention: I have them do nothing that they did not actually do when tested on this proving ground.

May I say, too, that much of what I put in this book was inspired by the grotesque prices paid for works of art during the past century. Tremendous concentrations of paper wealth have made it possible for a few persons or institutions to endow certain sorts of human playfulness with inappropriate and hence distressing seriousness. I think not only of the mudpies of art, but of children's games as well—running, jumping, catching, throwing.

Or dancing.

Or singing songs.

K.V.

"We are here to help each other get through this thing, whatever it is."

—Dr. Mark Vonnegut, M.D.
(Letter to Author, 1985)

Bluebeard

THE AUTOBIOGRAPHY OF
RABO KARABEKIAN
(1916-1988)

This book is for Circe Berman. What else can I say?

—R.K.

1

Having written "The End" to this story of my life, I find it prudent to scamper back here to before the beginning, to my front door, so to speak, and to make this apology to arriving guests: "I promised you an autobiography, but something went wrong in the kitchen. It turns out to be a *diary* of this past troubled summer, too! We can always send out for pizzas if necessary. Come *in,* come *in.*"

* * *

I am the erstwhile American painter Rabo Karabekian, a one-eyed man. I was born of immigrant parents in San Ignacio, California, in 1916. I begin this autobiography seventy-one years later. To those unfamiliar with the ancient mysteries of arithmetic, that makes this year 1987.

I was not born a cyclops. I was deprived of my left eye while commanding a platoon of Army Engineers, curiously enough artists of one sort or another in civilian life, in Luxembourg near the end of World War Two. We were specialists in camouflage, but at that time were fighting for our lives as ordinary infantry. The unit was composed of artists, since it was the theory of someone in the Army that we would be especially good at camouflage.

And so we were! And we were! What hallucinations we gave the Germans as to what was dangerous to them behind our lines, and what was not. Yes, and we were allowed to live like artists, too, hilariously careless in matters of dress and military courtesy. We were never attached to a unit as quotidian as a division or even a corps. We were under orders which came directly from the Supreme Headquarters of the Allied Expeditionary Force, which assigned us temporarily to this or that general, who had heard of our astonishing illusions. He was our patron for just a little while, permissive and fascinated and finally grateful.

Then off we went again.

Since I had joined the regular Army and become a lieutenant two years before the United States backed into the war, I might have attained the rank of lieutenant colonel at least by the end of the war. But I refused all promotions beyond captain in order to remain with my happy family of thirty-six men. That was my first experience with a family that large. My second came after the war, when I found myself a friend and seeming peer of those American painters who have now entered art history as founders of the Abstract Expressionist school.

* * *

My mother and father had families bigger than those two of mine back in the Old World—and of course their relatives back there were *blood* relatives. They lost their blood relatives to a massacre by the Turkish Empire of about one million of its Armenian citizens, who were thought to be treacherous for two reasons: first because they were clever and educated, and second because so many of them had relatives on the other side of Turkey's border with its enemy, the Russian Empire.

It was an age of Empires. So is this one, not all that well disguised.

* * *

The German Empire, allied with the Turks, sent impassive military observers to evaluate this century's first genocide, a word which did not exist in any language then. The word is now understood everywhere to mean a carefully planned effort to kill every member, be it man, woman, or child, of a perceived subfamily of the human race.

The problems presented by such ambitious projects are purely industrial: how to kill that many big, resourceful animals cheaply and quickly, make sure that nobody gets away, and dispose of mountains of meat and bones afterwards. The Turks, in their pioneering effort, had neither the aptitude for really big business nor the specialized machinery required. The Germans would exhibit both par excellence only one quarter of a century later. The Turks simply took all the Armenians they could find in their homes or places of work or refreshment or play or worship or education or whatever, marched them out into the countryside, and kept them away from food and water and shelter, and shot and bashed them and so on until they all appeared to be dead. It was up to dogs and vultures and rodents and so on, and finally worms, to clean up the mess afterwards.

My mother, who wasn't yet my mother, only pretended to be dead among the corpses.

My father, who wasn't yet her husband, hid in the shit and piss of a privy behind the schoolhouse where he was a teacher when the soldiers came. The school day was over, and my father-to-be was all alone in the schoolhouse writing poetry, he told me one time. Then he heard the soldiers coming and understood what they meant to do. Father never saw or heard the actual killing. For him, the stillness of the village, of which he was the only inhabitant at nightfall, all covered with shit and piss, was his most terrible memory of the massacre.

* * *

Although my mother's memories from the Old World were more gruesome than my father's, since she was right there in the killing fields, she somehow managed to put the massacre behind her and find much to like in the United States, and to daydream about a family future here.

My father *never* did.

* * *

I am a widower. My wife, née Edith Taft, who was my second such, died two years ago. She left me this nineteen-room house on the waterfront of East Hampton, Long Island, which had been in her Anglo-Saxon family from Cincinnati, Ohio, for three generations. Her ancestors surely never expected it to fall into the hands of a man with a name as exotic as Rabo Karabekian.

If they haunt this place, they do it with such Episcopalian good manners that no one has so far noticed them. If I were to come upon the spook of one of them on the grand staircase, and he or she indicated that I had no rights to this house, I would say this to him or her: "Blame the Statue of Liberty."

* * *

Dear Edith and I were happily married for twenty years. She was a grandniece of William Howard Taft, the twenty-seventh president of the United States and the tenth chief justice of the Supreme Court. She was the widow of a Cincinnati sportsman and investment banker named Richard Fairbanks, Jr., himself descended from Charles Warren Fairbanks, a United States senator from Indiana and then vice-president under Theodore Roosevelt.

We came to know each other long before her husband died when I persuaded her, and him, too, although this was her property, not his, to rent their unused potato barn to me for a studio. They had never been potato farmers, of course. They had simply bought land from a farmer next door, to the north, away from the beach, in order to keep it from being developed. With it had come the potato barn.

Edith and I did not come to know each other well

until after her husband died and my first wife, Dorothy, and our two sons, Terry and Henri, moved out on me. I sold our house, which was in the village of Springs, six miles north of here, and made Edith's barn not only my studio but my home.

That improbable dwelling, incidentally, is invisible from the main house, where I am writing now.

*   *   *

Edith had no children by her first husband, and she was past childbearing when I transmogrified her from being Mrs. Richard Fairbanks, Jr., into being Mrs. Rabo Karabekian instead.

So we were a very tiny family indeed in this great big house, with its two tennis courts and swimming pool, and its carriage house and its potato barn—and its three hundred yards of private beach on the open Atlantic Ocean.

One might think that my two sons, Terry and Henri Karabekian, whom I named in honor of my closest friend, the late Terry Kitchen, and the artist Terry and I most envied, Henri Matisse, might enjoy coming here with their families. Terry has two sons of his own now. Henri has a daughter.

But they do not speak to me.

"So be it! So be it!" I cry in this manicured wilderness. "Who gives a damn!" Excuse this outburst.

*   *   *

Dear Edith, like all great Earth Mothers, was a multitude. Even when there were only the two of us and the servants here, she filled this Victorian ark with love and merriment and hands-on domesticity. As privileged as she had been all her life, she cooked with the cook, gardened with the gardener, did all our food shopping, fed the pets and birds, and made personal friends of wild rabbits and squirrels and raccoons.

But we used to have a lot of parties, too, and guests who sometimes stayed for weeks—*her* friends and relatives, mostly. I have already said how matters stood and stand with my own few blood relatives, alienated descendants all. As for my synthetic relatives in the Army: some were killed in the little battle in which I was taken prisoner, and which cost me one eye. Those who survived I have never seen or heard from since. It may be that they were not as fond of me as I was of them.

These things happen.

The members of my other big synthetic family, the Abstract Expressionists, are mostly dead now, having been killed by everything from mere old age to suicide. The few survivors, like my blood relatives, no longer speak to me.

"So be it! So be it!" I cry in this manicured wilderness. "Who gives a damn!" Excuse this outburst.

*   *   *

All of our servants quit soon after Edith died. They said it had simply become too lonely here. So I hired some new ones, paying them a great deal of money to put up with me and all the loneliness. When Edith was alive, and the house was alive, the gardener and the two maids and the cook all lived here. Now only the cook, and, as I say, a different cook, lives in, and has the entire servants' quarters on the third floor of the ell to herself and her fifteen-year-old daughter. She is a divorced woman, a native of East Hampton, about forty, I would say. Her daughter, Celeste, does no work for me, but simply lives here and eats my food, and entertains her loud and willfully ignorant friends on my tennis courts and in my swimming pool and on my private oceanfront.

She and her friends ignore me, as though I were a senile veteran from some forgotten war, daydreaming away what little remains of his life as a museum guard. Why should I be offended? This house, in addition to being a home, shelters what is the most important collection of Abstract Expressionist paintings still in private hands. Since I have done no useful work for decades, what else am I, really, but a museum guard?

And, just as a paid museum guard would have to do, I answer as best I can the question put to me by visitor after visitor, stated in various ways, of course: "What are these pictures supposed to *mean*?"

* * *

These paintings, which are about absolutely nothing but themselves, were my own property long before I married Edith. They are worth at least as much as all the real estate and stocks and bonds, including a one-quarter share in the Cincinnati Bengals professional football team, which Edith left to me. So I cannot be stigmatized as an American fortune-hunter.

I may have been a lousy painter, but what a *collector* I turned out to be!

2

It has been very lonely here since Edith died. The friends we had were hers, not mine. Painters shun me, since the ridicule my own paintings attracted and deserved encouraged Philistines to argue that *most* painters were charlatans or fools. But I can stand loneliness, if I have to.

I stood it when a boy. I stood it for several years in New York City during the Great Depression. And after my first wife and my two sons left me in 1956, and I gave up on myself as a painter, I actually went looking for loneliness and found it. I was a hermit for eight years. How is that for a full-time job for a wounded vet?

* * *

And I *do* have a friend who is mine, all mine. He is the novelist Paul Slazinger, a wounded World War Two geezer like myself. He sleeps alone in a house next door to *my* old house in Springs.

I say he *sleeps* there, because he comes over *here* almost every day, and is probably on the property somewhere at this very moment, watching a tennis game, or sitting on the beach, staring out to sea, or playing cards with the cook in the kitchen, or hiding from everybody and everything, and reading a book where practically nobody ever goes, on the far side of the potato barn.

I don't think he writes much anymore. And, as I say, I don't paint at *all* anymore. I won't even doodle on the memo pad next to the downstairs telephone. A couple of weeks ago, I caught myself doing exactly that, and I deliberately snapped the point off the pencil, broke the pencil in two, and I threw its broken body into a wastebasket, like a baby rattlesnake which had wanted to *poison* me.

* * *

Paul has no money. He eats supper with me here four or five times a week, and gobbles directly from my refrigerator and fruit bowls during the daytime, so I am surely his primary source of nutriment. I have said to him many times after supper, "Paul—why don't you sell your house and get a little walking-around money, and move in here? Look at all the *room* I've got. And I'm never going to have a wife or a lady friend again, and neither are you. Jesus! Who would have us? We look like a couple of gutshot iguanas! So move in! I won't bother you, and you won't bother me. What could make more sense?"

His answer never varies much from this one: "I can only write at home." Some home, with a busted refrigerator and nobody ever there but him.

One time he said about this house: "Who could write in a museum?"

Well—I am now finding out if that can be done or not. I am *writing* in this museum.

Yes, it's true: I, old Rabo Karabekian, having disgraced myself in the visual arts, am now having a go at literature. A true child of the Great Depression, though, playing it safe, I am hanging on to my job as a museum guard.

What has inspired this amazing career change by one so old? *Cherchez la femme!*

Uninvited, as nearly as I can remember, an energetic and opinionated and voluptuous and relatively young woman has moved in with me!

She said she couldn't bear seeing and hearing me do absolutely nothing all day long—so why didn't I *do* something, do *anything*? If I couldn't think of anything else to do, why didn't I write my autobiography?

Why not, indeed?

She is so *authoritative!*

I find myself doing whatever she says I must do. During our twenty years of marriage, my dear Edith never *once* thought of something for me to do. In the Army, I knew several colonels and generals like this new woman in my life, but they were *men*, and we were a nation at war.

Is this woman a friend? I don't know what the hell she

is. All I know is that she isn't going to leave again until she's good and ready, and that she scares the *pants* off me.

Help.

Her name is Circe Berman.

* * *

She is a widow. Her husband was a brain surgeon in Baltimore, where she still has a house as big and empty as this one. Her husband Abe died of a brain hemorrhage six months ago. She is forty-three years old, and she has selected this house as a nice place to live and work while she writes her husband's biography.

There is nothing erotic about our relationship. I am twenty-eight years Mrs. Berman's senior, and have become too ugly for anyone but a dog to love. I really do look like a gutshot iguana, and am one-eyed besides. Enough is enough.

Here is how we met: she wandered onto my private beach alone one afternoon, not knowing it was private. She had never heard of me, since she hates modern art. She didn't know a soul in the Hamptons, and was staying in the Maidstone Inn in the village about a mile and a half from here. She had walked from there to the public beach, and then across my border.

I went down for my afternoon dip, and there she was, fully dressed, and doing what Paul Slazinger does so much of: sitting on sand and staring out to sea. The only reason I minded her being there, or anybody's being there, was my ludicrous physique and the fact I would have to take off my eye patch before I went in. There's quite a mess under there, not unlike a scrambled egg. I was embarrassed to be seen up close.

Paul Slazinger says, incidentally, that the human condition can be summed up in just one word, and this is the word: *Embarrassment.*

* * *

So I elected not to swim, but to sunbathe some distance away from her.

I did, however, come close enough to say, "Hello."

This was her curious reply: "Tell me how your parents died."

What a spooky woman! She could be a *witch.* Who but a witch could have persuaded me to write my autobiography?

She has just stuck her head in the room to say that it was time I went to New York City, where I haven't been since Edith died. I've hardly been out of this house since Edith died.

New York City, here I come. This is terrible!

* * *

"Tell me how your parents died," she said. I couldn't believe my ears.

"I beg your pardon?" I said.

"What good is 'Hello'?" she said.

She had stopped me in my tracks. "I've always thought it was better than nothing," I said, "but I could be wrong."

"What does 'Hello' mean?" she said.

And I said, "I had always understood it to mean 'Hello.'"

"Well it doesn't," she said. "It means, 'Don't talk about anything important.' It means, 'I'm smiling but not listening, so just go away.'"

She went on to avow that she was tired of just pretending to meet people. "So sit down here," she said, "and tell Mama how your parents died."

"Tell *Mama!*" Can you *beat* it?

She had straight black hair and large brown eyes like my mother—but she was much taller than my mother, and a little bit taller than me, for that matter. She was also much shapelier than my mother, who let herself become quite heavy, and who didn't care much what her hair looked like, either, or her clothes. Mother didn't care because Father didn't care.

And I told Mrs. Berman this about my mother: "She died when I was twelve—of a tetanus infection she evidently picked up while working in a cannery in California. The cannery was built on the site of an old livery stable, and tetanus bacteria often colonize the intestines of horses without hurting them, and then become durable spores, armored little seeds, when excreted. One of them lurking in the dirt around and under the cannery was somehow exhumed and sent traveling. After a long, long sleep it awakened in Paradise, something we would all like to do. Paradise was a cut in my mother's hand."

"So long, Mama," said Circe Berman.

There was that word *Mama* again.

"At least she didn't have to endure the Great Depression, which was only one year away," I said.

And at least she didn't have to see her only child come home a cyclops from World War Two.

"And how did your father die?" she said.

"In the Bijou Theater in San Ignacio in 1938," I said. "He went to the movie alone. He never even considered remarrying."

He still lived over the little store in California where he had got his first foothold in the economy of the United States of America. I had been living in Manhattan for five years then—and was working as an artist for an advertising agency. When the movie was over, the lights came on, and everybody went home but Father.

"What was the movie?" she asked.

And I said, *"Captains Courageous,* starring Spencer Tracy and Freddie Bartholomew."

*   *   *

What Father might have made of that movie, which was about cod fishermen in the North Atlantic, God only knows. Maybe he didn't see any of it before he died. If he did see some of it, he must have gotten rueful satisfaction from its having absolutely nothing to do with anything he had ever seen or anybody he had ever known. He welcomed all proofs that the planet he had known and loved during his boyhood had disappeared entirely.

That was *his* way of honoring all the friends and relatives he had lost in the massacre.

*   *   *

You *could* say that he became his own Turk over here, knocking himself down and spitting on himself. He could have studied English and become a respected teacher there in San Ignacio, and started writing poetry again, or maybe translated the Armenian poets he loved so much into English. But that wasn't *humiliating* enough. Nothing would do but that he, with all his education, become what his father and grandfather had been, which was a cobbler.

He was good at that craft, which he had learned as a boy, and which I would learn as a boy. But how he *complained*! At least he pitied himself in Armenian, which only Mother and I could understand. There weren't any other Armenians within a hundred miles of San Ignacio.

"I am looking for William Shakespeare, your greatest poet," he might say as he worked. *"Have you ever heard of him?"* He knew Shakespeare backwards and forwards in Armenian, and would often quote him. "To be or not to be . . ." for example, as far as he was concerned, was, *"Linel kam chlinel . . ."*

"Tear out my tongue if you catch me speaking Armenian," he might say. That was the penalty the Turks set in the seventeenth century for speaking any language but Turkish: a ripped-out tongue.

"Who are those people and what am I doing here?" he might say, with cowboys and Chinese and Indians passing by outside.

"When is San Ignacio going to erect a statue of Mesrob Mashtots?" he might say. Mesrob Mashtots was the inventor of the Armenian alphabet, unlike any other, about four hundred years before the birth of Christ. Armenians, incidentally, were the first people to make Christianity their national religion.

"One million, one million, one million," he might say. This is the generally accepted figure for the number of Armenians killed by the Turks in the massacre from which my parents escaped. That was two thirds of Turkey's Armenians, and about half the Armenians in the whole wide world. There are about six million of us now, including my two sons and three grandchildren,

who know nothing and care nothing about Mesrob
Mashtots.

"Musa Dagh!" he might say. This was the name of a
place in Turkey where a small band of Armenian civilians fought Turkish militiamen to a standstill for forty
days and forty nights before being exterminated—
about the time my parents, with me in my mother's
belly, arrived safe and sound in San Ignacio.

* * *

"Thank you, Vartan Mamigonian," he might say.
This was the name of a great Armenian national hero,
who led a losing army against the Persians in the fifth
century. The Vartan Mamigonian Father had in mind,
however, was an Armenian shoe manufacturer in
Cairo, Egypt, to which polyglot metropolis my parents
escaped after the massacre. It was he, a survivor of an
earlier massacre, who persuaded my naive parents,
who had met on a road to Cairo, that they would find
the streets paved with gold, if only they could find their
way to, of all places, San Ignacio, California. But that is a
story I will tell at another time.

"If anybody has discovered what life is all about,"
Father might say, *"it is too late. I am no longer interested."*

*"Never is heard a discouraging word, and the skies
are not cloudy all day,"* he might say. These, of course,
are words from the American song "Home on the
Range," which he had translated into Armenian. He
found them idiotic.

"Tolstoi made shoes," he might say. This was a fact, of
course: the greatest of Russian writers and idealists had,
in an effort to do work that mattered, made shoes for a

little while. May I say that I, too, could make shoes if I had to.

*   *   *

Circe Berman says she can make *pants* if she has to. As she would tell me when we met on the beach, her father had a pants factory in Lackawanna, New York, until he went bankrupt and hanged himself.

*   *   *

If my father had managed to survive *Captains Courageous*, starring Spencer Tracy and Freddie Bartholomew, and had lived to see the paintings I did after the war, several of which drew serious critical attention, and a few of which I sold for what was quite a bit of money back then, he surely would have been among the great American majority which snorted and jeered at them. He wouldn't have razzed just me. He would have razzed my Abstract Expressionist pals, too, Jackson Pollock and Mark Rothko and Terry Kitchen and so on, painters who are now, unlike myself, acknowledged to be some of the most brilliant artists ever to have been produced not just by the United States but by the whole damn world. But what sticks in my mind like a thorn now, and I haven't thought about this for years: he would have had no hesitation in razzing his own son, in razzing me.

So, thanks to the conversation Mrs. Berman struck up with me on the beach only two weeks ago, I am in a frenzy of adolescent resentment against a father who was buried almost fifty years ago! Let me off this hellish time machine!

But there is no getting off this hellish time machine. I

have to think now, even though it is the last I would ever want to think about, if I had a choice, that my own father would have laughed as hard as anybody when my paintings, thanks to unforeseen chemical reactions between the sizing of my canvases and the acrylic wall-paint and colored tapes I had applied to them, all destroyed themselves.

I mean—people who had paid fifteen- or twenty- or even thirty thousand dollars for a picture of mine found themselves gazing at a blank canvas, all ready for a new picture, and ringlets of colored tapes and what looked like moldy Rice Krispies on the floor.

*   *   *

It was a postwar miracle that did me in. I had better explain to my young readers, if any, that the Second World War had many of the promised characteristics of Armageddon, a final war between good and evil, so that nothing would do but that it be followed by miracles. Instant coffee was one. DDT was another. It was going to kill all the bugs, and almost did. Nuclear energy was going to make electricity so cheap that it might not even be metered. It would also make another war unthinkable. Talk about loaves and fishes! Antibiotics would defeat all diseases. Lazarus would never die: How was that for a scheme to make the Son of God obsolete?

Yes, and there were miraculous breakfast foods and would soon be helicopters for every family. There were miraculous new fibers which could be washed in cold water and need no ironing afterwards! Talk about a war well worth fighting!

During that war we had a word for extreme man-

made disorder which was *fubar,* an acronym for
"fucked up beyond all recognition." Well—the whole
planet is now fubar with postwar miracles, but, back in
the early 1960s, I was one of the first persons to be
totally wrecked by one—an acrylic wall-paint whose
colors, according to advertisements of the day, would
". . . outlive the smile on the 'Mona Lisa.' "

The name of the paint was Sateen Dura-Luxe. Mona
Lisa is still smiling. And your local paint dealer, if he has
been in the business any length of time, will laugh in
your face if you ask for Sateen Dura-Luxe.

* * *

"Your father had the Survivor's Syndrome," said
Circe Berman to me on my beach that day. "He was
ashamed not to be dead like all his friends and relatives."

"He was ashamed that I wasn't dead, too," I said.

"Think of it as a noble emotion gone wrong," she
said.

"He was a very upsetting father," I said. "I'm sorry
now that you've made me remember him."

"As long as we've brought him back," she said, "why
don't you forgive him now?"

"I've done it a hundred times already," I said. "This
time I'm going to be smart and get a receipt." I went on
to assert that Mother was more entitled to Survivor's
Syndrome than Father, since she had been right in the
middle of the killing, pretending to be dead with people lying on top of her, and with screams and blood
everywhere. She wasn't all that much older then than
the cook's daughter, Celeste.

While Mother was lying there, she was looking right

into the face of the corpse of an old woman who had no teeth, only inches away. The old woman's mouth was open, and inside it and on the ground below it was a fortune in unset jewels.

"If it weren't for those jewels," I told Mrs. Berman, "I would not be a citizen of this great country, and would be in no position to tell you that you are now trespassing on my private property. That's my house there, on the other side of the dunes. Would you be offended if a lonely and harmless old widower invited you thence for a drink, if you drink, and then supper with an equally harmless old friend of mine?" I meant Paul Slazinger.

She accepted. And after supper I heard myself saying, "If you'd rather stay here instead of the inn, you're certainly welcome." And I made her the same guarantee I made many times to Slazinger: "I promise not to bother you."

So let's be honest. I said a little earlier that I had no idea how she had come to share this house with me. Let's be honest. I *invited* her.

3

She has turned me and this household upside down!

I should have known how manipulative she was from the very first words she ever said to me: "Tell me how your parents died." I mean—those were the words of a woman who was quite used to turning people in any direction she chose, as though they were machine bolts and she were a monkey wrench.

And if I had missed the warning signals on the beach, there were plenty more at supper. She behaved as though she were a paying customer in a fancy restaurant, screwing up her face after tasting a wine which I myself had sipped and declared potable, and declaring the veal to be overcooked and ordering Slazinger to send his serving back to the kitchen along with hers, and saying that she was going to plan the meals while she was here, since Paul's and my circulatory systems were obviously, since our complexions were so pasty and our gestures so listless, clogged up with cholesterol.

* * *

She was outrageous! She sat across from a Jackson Pollock for which I had just been offered two million dollars by an anonymous collector in Switzerland, and she said, "I wouldn't give that houseroom!"

So I asked her tartly, after a wink in Slazinger's direction, what sort of picture might please her more.

She replied that she wasn't on Earth to be pleased but to be instructed. "I need information the way I need vitamins and minerals," she said. "Judging from your pictures, you hate facts like poison."

"I suppose you would be happier looking at George Washington crossing the Delaware," I said.

"Who wouldn't?" she said. "But I tell you what I'd really like to see there since our talk on the beach."

"Which is—?" I said, arching my eyebrows and then winking at Slazinger again.

"I'd like a picture with some grass and dirt at the bottom," she said.

"Brown and green," I suggested.

"Fine," she said. "And sky at the top."

"Blue," I said.

"Maybe with clouds," she said.

"Easily supplied," I said.

"And in between the sky and the ground—" she said.

"A duck?" I said. "An organ-grinder with his monkey? A sailor and his girl on a park bench?"

"Not a duck and not an organ-grinder and not a sailor and his girl," she said. "A whole lot of dead bodies lying every which way on the ground. And very close to us is the face of a beautiful girl, maybe sixteen or seventeen. She is pinned under the corpse of a man, but she is still alive, and she is staring into the open mouth of a dead old woman whose face is only inches from hers. Out of that toothless mouth are spilling diamonds and emeralds and rubies."

There was a silence.

And then she said, "You could build a whole new religion, and a much needed one, too, on a picture like that." She nodded in the direction of the Pollock. "All anybody could do with a picture like that is illustrate an advertisement for a hangover remedy or seasick pills."

* * *

Slazinger asked her what had brought her to the Hamptons, since she didn't know anybody here. She replied that she hoped to find some peace and quiet so she could devote her full attention to writing a biography of her husband, the Baltimore brain surgeon.

Slazinger preened himself as a man who had published eleven novels and he patronized her as an amateur.

"Everybody thinks he or she can be a writer," he said with airy irony.

"Don't tell me it's a crime to try," she said.

"It's a crime to think it's easy," he said. "But if you're really serious, you'll find out quick enough that it's the hardest thing there is."

"Particularly so, if you have absolutely nothing to say," she said. "Don't you think that's the main reason people find it so difficult? If they can write complete sentences and can use a dictionary, isn't that the *only* reason they find writing hard: they don't know or care about anything?"

Here Slazinger stole a line from the writer Truman Capote, who died five years ago, and who had a house only a few miles west of here. "I think you're talking about *typing* instead of *writing*," he said.

She promptly identified the source of his witticism: "Truman Capote," she said.

Slazinger covered himself nicely. "As everyone knows," he said.

"If you didn't have such a kind face," she said, "I would suspect that you were making fun of me."

But listen to this, which she only told me at breakfast this morning. Just listen to this and then tell me who was toying with whom at that supper, which is now two weeks ago: Mrs. Berman is *not* an amateur writing a biography of her late husband. That was just a story to cover her true identity and purpose for being here. She swore me to secrecy, and then confessed that she was really in the Hamptons to research and write a novel about working-class adolescents living in a resort community teeming in the summer time with the sons and daughters of multimillionaires.

And this wasn't going to be her first novel either. It would be the twenty-first in a series of shockingly frank and enormously popular novels for young readers, several of which had been made into motion pictures. She had written them under the name of "Polly Madison."

* * *

I certainly *will* keep this a secret, too, if only to save the life of Paul Slazinger. If he finds out who she really is now, after all his posturing as a professional writer, he will do what Terry Kitchen, the only other best friend I ever had, did. He will commit suicide.

In terms of commercial importance in the literary marketplace, Circe Berman is to Paul Slazinger what General Motors is to a bicycle factory in Albania!

Mum's the word!

* * *

She said that first night that she collected pictures, too.

I asked her what kind, and she said, "Victorian chromos of little girls on swings." She said she had more than a hundred of them, all different, but all of little girls on swings.

"I suppose you think that's terrible," she said.

"Not at all," I said, "just as long as you keep them safely caged in Baltimore."

* * *

That first night, I remember, too, she asked Slazinger and me, and then the cook and her daughter, too, if we knew any true stories about local girls from relatively poor families who had married the sons of rich people.

Slazinger said, "I don't think you'll even see that in the *movies* anymore."

Celeste told her, "The rich marry the rich. Where have you *been* all your life?"

*   *   *

To get back to the past, which is what this book is supposed to be all about: My mother gathered up the jewels that had fallen from the dead woman's mouth, but not the ones still inside there. Whenever she told the story, she was emphatic about that: she hadn't fished anything from the woman's mouth. Whatever had stayed in there was still the woman's very personal property.

And Mother crawled away after nightfall, after the killers had all gone home. She wasn't from my father's village, and she would not meet him until they both crossed the lightly guarded border with Persia, about seventy miles from the scene of the massacre.

Persian Armenians took them in. After they decided to go together to Egypt. My father did most of the talking, since Mother had a mouthful of jewels. When they got to the Persian Gulf, mother sold the first of those compact treasures in order to buy them passage on a small freighter to Cairo, via the Red Sea. And it was in Cairo that they met the criminal Vartan Mamigonian, a survivor of an earlier massacre.

"Never trust a survivor," my father used to warn me, with Vartan Mamigonian in mind, "until you find out what he did to stay alive."

*   *   *

This Mamigonian had grown rich manufacturing military boots for the British Army and the German Army, which would soon be fighting each other in World War One. He offered my parents low-paid work of the dirtiest kind. They were fools enough to tell him, since he

was a fellow Armenian survivor, about Mother's jewels
and their plans to marry and go to Paris to join the large
and highly cultivated Armenian colony there.

Mamigonian became their most ardent advisor and
protector, eager to find them a safe place for the jewels
in a city notorious for its heartless thieves. But they had
already put them in a bank.

So Mamigonian constructed a fantasy which he pro-
posed to trade for the jewels. He must have found San
Ignacio, California, in an atlas, since no Armenian had
ever been there, and since no news of that sleepy farm-
ing town could have reached the Near East in any form.
Mamigonian said he had a brother in San Ignacio. He
forged letters from the brother to prove it. The letters
said, moreover, that the brother had become extremely
rich in a short time there. There were many other Armenians there, all doing well. They were looking for a
teacher for their children who was fluent in Armenian
and familiar with the great literature in that language.

As an inducement to such a teacher, they would sell
him a house and twenty acres of fruit trees at a fraction
of their true value. Mamigonian's "rich brother" en-
closed a photo of the house, and a deed to it as well.

If Mamigonian knew a good teacher in Cairo who
might be interested, this nonexistent brother wrote,
Mamigonian was authorized to sell him the deed. This
would secure the teaching job for Father, and make
him one of the larger property owners in idyllic San
Ignacio.

4

I have been in the art business, the picture business, so long now that I can daydream about the past as though it were a vista through a series of galleries like the Louvre, perhaps—home of the "Mona Lisa," whose smile has now outlived by three decades the postwar miracle of Sateen Dura-Luxe. The pictures in what must be the final gallery of my life are real. I can touch them, if I like, or, following the recommendations of the widow Berman, a.k.a. "Polly Madison," sell them to the highest bidder or in some other way, in her thoughtful words, "Get them the hell out of here."

In the imaginary galleries in the distance are my own Abstract Expressionist paintings, miraculously resurrected by the Great Critic for Judgment Day, and then pictures by Europeans, which I bought for a few dollars or chocolate bars or nylon stockings when a soldier, and then advertisements of the sort I had been laying out and illustrating before I joined the Army—at about the time news of my father's death in the Bijou Theater in San Ignacio came.

Still farther away are the magazine illustrations of Dan Gregory, whose apprentice I was from the time I was seventeen until he threw me out. I was one month short of being twenty when he threw me out. Beyond the Dan Gregory Gallery are unframed works I made in my boyhood, as the only artist of any age or sort ever to inhabit San Ignacio.

The gallery at the farthest remove from me in my dotage, though, just inside the door I entered in 1916, is devoted to a photograph, not a painting. Its subject is a noble white house with a long winding driveway and porte-cochère, supposedly in San Ignacio, which Vartan Mamigonian in Cairo told my parents they were buying with most of Mother's jewelry.

That picture, along with a bogus deed, crawling with signatures and spattered with sealing wax, was in my parents' bedside table for many years—in the tiny apartment over Father's shoe repair shop. I assumed that he had thrown them out with so many other mementos after Mother died. But as I was about to board a railroad train in 1933, to seek my fortune in New York City during the depths of the Great Depression, Father made me a present of the photograph. "If you happen to come across this house," he said in Armenian, "let me know where it is. Wherever it is, it belongs to me."

* * *

I don't own that picture anymore. Coming back to New York City after having been one of three persons at Father's funeral in San Ignacio, which I hadn't seen for five years, I ripped the photograph to bits. I did that because I was angry at my dead father. It was my conclusion that he had cheated himself and my mother a lot worse than they had been cheated by Vartan Mamigonian. It wasn't Mamigonian who made my parents stay in San Ignacio instead of moving to Fresno, say, where there really *was* an Armenian colony, whose members supported each other and kept the old language and customs and religion alive, and at the same time became happier and happier to be in California. Father could have become a beloved teacher again!

Oh, no—it wasn't Mamigonian who tricked him into being the unhappiest and loneliest of all the world's cobblers.

* * *

Armenians have done brilliantly in this country during the short time they've been here. My neighbor to the west is F. Donald Kasabian, executive vice-president of Metropolitan Life—so that right here in exclusive East Hampton, and right on the beach, too, we have *two* Armenians side by side. What used to be J. P. Morgan's estate in Southampton is now the property of Kevork Hovanessian, who also owned Twentieth Century-Fox until he sold it last week.

And Armenians haven't succeeded only in business

here. The great writer William Saroyan was an Armenian, and so is Dr. George Mintouchian, the new president of the University of Chicago. Dr. Mintouchian is a
renowned Shakespeare scholar, something my father
could have been.

And Circe Berman has just come into the room and
read what is in my typewriter, which is ten of the lines
above. She is gone again. She said again that my father
obviously suffered from Survivor's Syndrome.

"Everybody who is alive is a survivor, and everybody
who is dead isn't," I said. "So everybody alive must have
the Survivor's Syndrome. It's that or death. I am so
damn sick of people telling me proudly that they are
survivors! Nine times out of ten it's a cannibal or billion-
aire!"

"You still haven't forgiven your father for being what
he had to be," she said. "That's why you're yelling
now."

"I wasn't yelling," I said.

"They can hear you in Portugal," she said. That's
where you wind up if you put out to sea from my private beach and sail due east, as she had figured out from
the globe in the library. You wind up in Oporto, Portugal.

"You envy your father's ordeal," she said.

"I had an ordeal of my own!" I said. "In case you
haven't noticed, I'm a one-eyed man."

"You told me yourself that there was almost no pain,
and that it healed right away," she said, which was true.
I don't remember being hit, but only the approach of a
white German tank and German soldiers all in white
across a snow-covered meadow in Luxembourg. I was
unconscious when I was taken prisoner, and was kept

that way by morphine until I woke up in a German military hospital in a church across the border, in Germany. She was right: I had to endure no more pain in the war than a civilian experiences in a dentist's chair.

The wound healed so quickly that I was soon shipped off to a camp as just another unremarkable prisoner.

*   *   *

Still, I insisted that I was as entitled to a Survivor's Syndrome as my father, so she asked me two questions. The first one was this: "Do you believe sometimes that you are a good person in a world where almost all of the other good people are dead?"

"No," I said.

"Do you sometimes believe that you must be wicked, since all the good people are dead, and that the only way to clear your name is to be dead, too?"

"No," I said.

"You may be entitled to the Survivor's Syndrome, but you didn't get it," she said. "Would you like to try for tuberculosis instead?"

*   *   *

"How do you know so much about the Survivor's Syndrome?" I asked her. This wasn't a boorish question to ask her, since she had told me during our first meeting on the beach that she and her husband, although both Jewish, had had no knowledge of relatives they might have had in Europe and who might have been killed during the Holocaust. They were both from families which had been in the United States for several generations, and which had lost all contact with European relatives.

"I wrote a book about it," she said. "Rather—I wrote about people like you: children of a parent who had survived some sort of mass killing. It's called *The Underground*."

Needless to say, I have not read that or any of the Polly Madison books, although they seem, now that I have started looking around for them, as available as packs of chewing gum.

* * *

Not that I would need to leave the house to get a copy of *The Underground* or any other Polly Madison book, Mrs. Berman informs me. The cook's daughter Celeste has every one of them.

Mrs. Berman, the most ferocious enemy of privacy I ever knew, has also discovered that Celeste, although only *fifteen,* already takes birth-control pills.

* * *

The formidable widow Berman told me the plot of *The Underground,* which is this: Three girls, one black, one Jewish and one Japanese, feel drawn together and separate from the rest of their classmates for reasons they can't explain. They form a little club which they call, again for reasons they can't explain, "The Underground."

But then it turns out that all three have a parent or grandparent who has survived some man-made catastrophe, and who, without meaning to, passed on to them the idea that the wicked were the living and that the good were dead.

The black is descended from a survivor of the massacre of Ibos in Nigeria. The Japanese is a descendant of a survivor of the atom-bombing of Nagasaki. The Jew is a descendant of a survivor of the Nazi Holocaust.

* * *

"*The Underground* is a wonderful title for a book like that," I said.

"You bet it is," she said. "I am very proud of my titles." She really thinks that she is the cat's pajamas, and that everybody else is dumb, dumb, dumb!

* * *

She said that painters should hire writers to name their pictures for them. The names of the pictures on my walls here are "Opus Nine" and "Blue and Burnt Orange" and so on. My own most famous painting, which no longer exists, and which was sixty-four feet long and eight feet high, and used to grace the entrance lobby of the GEFFCo headquarters on Park Avenue, was called simply, "Windsor Blue Number Seventeen." Windsor Blue was a shade of Sateen Dura-Luxe, straight from the can.

"The titles are *meant* to be uncommunicative," I said.

"What's the point of being alive," she said, "if you're not going to *communicate?*"

She still has no respect for my art collection, although, during the five weeks she has now been in residence, she has seen immensely respectable people from as far away as Switzerland and Japan worship some of them as though the pictures were gods almost. She was here when I sold a Rothko right off the wall to a man from the Getty Museum for a million and a half dollars.

What she said about that was this: "Good riddance of bad rubbish. It was rotting your brain because it was about absolutely nothing. Now give the rest of them the old heave-ho!"

*　*　*

She asked me just now, while we were talking about the Survivor's Syndrome, if my father wanted to see the Turks punished for what they had done to the Armenians.

"I asked him the same thing when I was about eight years old, I guess, and thinking maybe life would be spicier if we wanted revenge of some kind," I said.

"Father put down his tools there in his little shop, and he stared out the window," I went on, "and I looked out the window, too. There were a couple of Luma Indian men out there, I remember. The Luma reservation was only five miles away, and sometimes people passing through town would mistake me for a Luma boy. I liked that a lot. At the time I thought it certainly beat being an Armenian.

"Father finally answered my question this way: 'All I want from the Turks is an admission that their country is an uglier and even more joyless place, now that *we* are gone.' "

*　*　*

I went for a manly tramp around my boundaries after lunch today, and encountered my neighbor to the north on our mutual border, which runs about twenty feet north of my potato barn. His name is John Karpinski. He is a native. He is a potato farmer like his father, although his fields must now be worth about eighty thousand dollars an acre, since the second-story windows of houses built on them would have an ocean view. Three generations of Karpinskis have been raised on all that property, so that to them, in an Armenian manner of speaking, it is their own sacred ancestral bit of ground at the foot of Mount Ararat.

Karpinski is a huge man, almost always in bib-overalls, and everybody calls him "Big John." Big John is a wounded war veteran like Paul Slazinger and me, but he is younger than us, so his war was a different war. His war was the Korean War.

And then his only son "Little John" was killed by a land mine in the Vietnam War.

One war to a customer.

* * *

My potato barn and the six acres that came with it used to belong to Big John's father, who sold them to Dear Edith and her first husband.

Big John expressed curiosity about Mrs. Berman. I promised him that our relationship was platonic, and that she had more or less invited herself, and that I would be glad when she returned to Baltimore.

"She sounds like a bear," he said. "If a bear gets in your house, you had better go to a motel until the bear is ready to leave again."

There used to be lots of bears on Long Island, but there certainly aren't bears anymore. He said his knowledge of bears came from his father, who, at the age of sixty, was treed by a grizzly in Yellowstone Park. After that, John's father read every book about bears he could get his hands on.

"I'll say this for that bear—" said John, "it got the old man reading books again."

* * *

Mrs. Berman is so God damn nosy! I mean—she comes in here and reads what is in my typewriter without feeling the need to ask permission first.

"How come you never use semicolons?" she'll say. Or: "How come you chop it all up into little sections instead of letting it flow and flow?" *That* sort of thing.

And when I listen to her moving about this house, I not only hear her footsteps: I hear the opening and closing of drawers and cupboards, too. She has investigated every nook and cranny, including the basement. She came up from the basement one day and said, "Do you know you've got sixty-three gallons of Sateen Dura-Luxe down there?" She had *counted* them!

It is against the law to dispose of Sateen Dura-Luxe in an ordinary dump because it has been found to degrade over time into a very deadly poison. To get rid of the stuff legally, I would have to ship it to a special disposal area near Pitchfork, Wyoming, and I have never got around to doing that. So there it sits in the basement after all these years.

* * *

The one place on the property she hasn't explored is my studio, the potato barn. It is a very long and narrow structure without windows, with sliding doors and a potbellied stove at either end, built for the storage of potatoes and nothing else. The idea was this: a farmer might maintain an even temperature in there, no matter what the weather, with the stoves and the doors, so that his potatoes would neither freeze nor sprout until he was ready to market them.

It was structures with such unusual dimensions, in fact, along with what used to be very cheap property, which caused many painters to move out here when I was young, and especially painters who were working on exceptionally large canvases. I would never have been able to work on the eight panels comprising "Windsor Blue Number Seventeen" as a single piece, if I hadn't rented that potato barn.

*   *   *

The nosy widow Berman, a.k.a. "Polly Madison," can't get into the studio or even take a peek inside because it has no windows and because two years ago, right after my wife died, I personally nailed the doors at one end shut from the inside with six-inch spikes, and immobilized the doors at the other end on the outside, from top to bottom, with six big padlocks and massive hasps.

I myself haven't been in there since. And, yes, there is something in there. This is no shaggy dog story. After I die and am buried next to my darling Edith, and the executors of my estate open those doors at last, they will find more than just thin air in there. And it won't be some pathetic symbol, such as a paintbrush broken in two or my Purple Heart on an otherwise vacant and clean-swept floor.

And there is no lame joke in there, like a painting of potatoes, as though I were returning the barn to potatoes, or a painting of the Virgin Mary wearing a derby and holding a watermelon, or some such thing.

And no self-portrait.

And nothing with a religious message.

Tantalizing? Here's a hint: it's bigger than a bread box and smaller than the planet Jupiter.

* * *

Not even Paul Slazinger has come close to guessing what is in there, and he has said more than once that he doesn't see how our friendship can continue, if I feel my secret would not be safe with him.

The barn has become quite famous in the art world. After I show visitors the collection in the house, most of them ask if they can see what is in the barn as well. I tell them that they can see the outside of the barn, if they like, and that the outside is in fact a significant landmark in art history. The first time Terry Kitchen used a paint-spraying rig, his target was an old piece of beaverboard he had leaned against the barn.

"As for what's *inside* the barn," I tell them, "it's the worthless secret of a silly old man, as the world will discover when I have gone to the big art auction in the sky."

5

One art publication claimed to know *exactly* what was in there: the very greatest of the Abstract Expressionist paintings, which I was keeping off the market in order to raise the value of relatively unimportant paintings in the house here.

Not true.

*　*　*

After that article was printed, my fellow Armenian in Southampton, Kevork Hovanissian, made a serious offer of three million dollars for everything in the barn, sight unseen.

"I wouldn't want to cheat you that way," I told him. "That would be un-Armenian."

If I had taken his money, it would have been like selling him Brooklyn Bridge.

* * *

One response to that same article wasn't that amusing. A man whose name I did not recognize, said in a letter to the editor that he had known me during the war, which he evidently did. He was at least familiar with my platoon of artists, which he described accurately. He knew the mission we were given after the German Air Force had been knocked out of the sky and there was no longer any need for the big-time camouflage jokes we played. This was the mission, which was like turning children loose in the workshop of Father Christmas: we were to evaluate and catalogue all captured works of art.

This man said he had served in SHAEF, and I must have dealt with him from time to time. It was his belief, as stated in his letter, that I had stolen masterpieces which should have been returned to their rightful owners in Europe. Fearing lawsuits brought by those rightful owners, he said, I had locked them up in the barn.

Wrong.

* * *

He is wrong about the contents of the barn. I have to say he is just a little bit right about my having taken advantage of my unusual wartime opportunities. I couldn't have stolen anything which was handed over by the military units which had captured it. I had to give them receipts, and we were visited regularly by auditors from the Finance Corps.

But our travels behind the lines *did* bring us into contact with persons in desperate circumstances who had art to sell. We got some remarkable *bargains.*

Nobody in the platoon got an Old Master, or anything which obviously came from a church or a museum or a great private collection. At least I don't *think* anybody did. I can't be absolutely sure about that. In the Art World, as elsewhere, opportunists are opportunists and thieves are thieves.

But I myself *did* buy from a civilian an unsigned charcoal sketch which looked like a Cézanne to me, and which has since been authenticated as such. It is now a part of the permanent collection of the Rhode Island School of Design. And I bought a Matisse, my favorite painter, from a widow who said her husband had been given it by the artist himself. For that matter, I got stuck with a fake Gauguin, which served me right.

And I sent my purchases for safekeeping to just about the only person I knew and could trust in the whole United States of America anymore, Sam Wu, a Chinese laundryman in New York City who was a cook for a little while for my former master, the illustrator Dan Gregory.

Imagine fighting for a country where the only civilian you know is a Chinese laundryman!

And then one day I and my platoon of artists were ordered into combat, to contain, if we could, the last big German breakthrough of World War Two.

*   *   *

But none of that stuff is in the barn, or even in my possession. I sold it all when I got home from the war, which gave me a nice little bankroll to invest in the stock market. I had given up my boyhood dream of being an artist. I enrolled in courses in accounting and economics and business law and marketing and so on at New York University. I was going to be a *businessman.*

I thought this about myself and art: that I could catch the likeness of anything I could see—with patience and the best instruments and materials. I had, after all, been an able apprentice under the most meticulous illustrator of this century, Dan Gregory. But cameras could do what he had done and what I could do. And I knew that it was this same thought which had sent the Impressionists and the Cubists and the Dadaists and the Surrealists and so on in their quite successful efforts to make good pictures which cameras and people like Dan Gregory could not duplicate.

I concluded that my mind was so ordinary, which is to say empty, that I could never be anything but a reasonably good camera. So I would content myself with a more common and general sort of achievement than serious art, which was money. I was not saddened about this. I was in fact much *relieved!*

But I still enjoyed engaging in the blather of art, since I could talk if not paint pictures as well as anyone. So I would go to bars around NYU at night, and easily made friends with several painters who thought they were right about almost everything, but who never expected to receive much recognition. I could talk as well as the best of them, and drink as much as they could. Best of all, I could pick up the check at the end of the evening, thanks to the money I was making in the stock market, subsistence payments I was receiving from the government while going to the university, and a lifetime pension from a grateful nation for my having given one eye in defense of Liberty.

To the real painters I seemed a bottomless pit of money. I was good not only for the cost of drinks, but for rent, for a down payment on a car, for a girlfriend's abortion, for a wife's abortion. You name it. However much money they needed for no matter what, they could get it from Diamond Rabo Karabekian.

*   *   *

So I bought those friends. My pit of money wasn't really bottomless. By the end of every month they had taken me for everything I had. But then the pit, a small one, would fill up again.

Fair was fair. I certainly enjoyed their company, especially since they treated me as though I were a painter, too. I was one of them. Here was another big family to replace my lost platoon.

And they paid me back with more than companionship. They settled their debts as best they could with pictures nobody wanted, too.

*   *   *

I almost forgot to say: I was married and my wife was pregnant at the time. She would be *twice* impregnated by that incomparable lover, Rabo Karabekian.

*   *   *

I have now returned to this typewriter from the vicinity of the swimming pool, where I asked Celeste and her friends in and around that public teenage athletic facility, if they knew who Bluebeard was. I meant to mention Bluebeard in this book. I wanted to know if I had to explain, for the sake of young readers, who Bluebeard was.

Nobody knew. While I was at it, I asked them if they recognized the names of Jackson Pollock, Mark Rothko, or Terry Kitchen, or Truman Capote, or Nelson Algren, or Irwin Shaw, or James Jones, all of whom had figured not only in the history of arts and letters but in the history of the Hamptons. They did not. So much for achieving immortality via the arts and letters.

So: Bluebeard is a fictitious character in a very old children's tale, possibly based loosely on a murderous nobleman of long ago. In the story, he has married many times. He marries for the umpteenth time, and brings his latest child bride back to his castle. He tells her that she can go into any room but one, whose door he shows her.

Bluebeard is either a poor psychologist or a great one, since all his new wife can think about is what might be behind the door. So she takes a look when she thinks he isn't home, but he really *is* home.

He catches her just at the point she is gazing aghast at the bodies of all his former wives in there, all of whom he has murdered, save for the first one, for looking behind the door. The first one got murdered for something else.

*   *   *

So—of all the people who know about my locked potato barn, the one who finds the mystery most intolerable is surely Circe Berman. She is after me all the time to tell her where the six keys are, and I tell her again that they are buried in a golden casket at the foot of Mount Ararat.

I said to her the last time she asked, which was about five minutes ago: "Look: think about something else, anything else. I am Bluebeard, and my studio is my *forbidden chamber* as far as *you're* concerned."

6

The Bluebeard story notwithstanding, there are no bodies in my barn. The first of my two wives, who was and is Dorothy, remarried soon after our divorce, remarried *happily*, from all accounts. Dorothy is now a widow in a beachfront condominium in Sarasota, Florida. Her second husband was what we both thought I might become right after the war: a capable and personable insurance man. We each have a beach.

My second wife, dear Edith, is buried in Green River Cemetery out here, where I expect to be buried, too—only a few yards, in fact, from the graves of Jackson Pollock and Terry Kitchen.

If I killed anybody in the war, and I just might have, it would have been during the few seconds before a shell from somewhere knocked me unconscious and took out one eye.

*　*　*

When I was a two-eyed boy, I was the best draughts-man they had ever seen in the rinky-dink public school system of San Ignacio, which wasn't saying much. Several of my teachers were so impressed that they suggested to my parents that perhaps I should pursue a career as an artist.

But this advice seemed so impractical to my parents that they asked the teachers to stop putting such ideas in my head. They thought that artists lived in poverty, and that they had to die before their works were appreciated. They were generally right about that, of course. The paintings by dead men who were poor most of their lives are the most valuable pieces in my collection.

And if an artist wants to really jack up the prices of his creations, may I suggest this: suicide.

*　*　*

But in 1927, when I was eleven years old, and was incidentally well on my way to becoming as good a cobbler as my father, my mother read about an American artist who made as much money as many movie stars and tycoons, and was in fact the friend and equal of movie stars and tycoons, and had a yacht—and a horse farm in Virginia, and a beach house in Montauk, not far from here.

Mother would say later, and not all that much later, since she had only one more year to live, that she never would have read the article if it hadn't been for a photo-graph of this rich artist on his yacht. The name of the yacht was the name of the mountain as sacred to Arme-nians as Fujiyama is to the Japanese: *Ararat.*

This man had to be an Armenian, she thought, and so he was. The magazine said he had been born Dan Gre-gorian in Moscow, where his father was a horse trainer, and that he had been apprenticed to the chief engraver of the Russian Imperial Mint.

He had come to this country in 1907 as an ordinary immigrant, not a refugee from any massacre, and had changed his name to Dan Gregory, and had become an illustrator of magazine stories and advertisements, and of books for young people. The author of the article said he was probably the highest paid artist in American history.

That could still be true of Dan Gregory, or "Grego-rian," as my parents always called him, if his income in the 1920s, or especially during the Great Depression, were translated into the depreciated dollars of today. He could still be the champ, living or dead.

* * *

My mother was shrewd about the United States, as my father was not. She had figured out that the most pervasive American disease was loneliness, and that even people at the top often suffered from it, and that they could be surprisingly responsive to attractive strangers who were friendly.

So my mother said to me, and I hardly recognized her, so sly and witchlike had her face become: "You must *write* to this Gregorian. You must tell him that you are also Armenian. You must tell him that you want to be an artist half as good as he is, and that you think he is the greatest artist who ever lived."

*   *   *

So I wrote such a letter, or about twenty such letters, in my childish longhand, until Mother was satisfied that the bait was irresistible. I did this hard work in an acrid cloud of my father's raillery.

He said things like "He stopped being an Armenian when he changed his name," and "If he grew up in Moscow, he's a Russian not an Armenian," and "You know what a letter like that would mean to me? 'The next one asks for money.' "

And Mother said to him in Armenian: "Can't you see we're fishing? If you make so much noise talking, you'll scare the fish away."

In Turkish Armenia, incidentally, or so I've been told, it was the women and not the men who were the fisherfolk.

And what a terrific bite my letter got!

We hooked Dan Gregory's mistress, a former Ziegfeld Follies showgirl named Marilee Kemp!

This woman would become the very first woman I ever made love to—at the age of *nineteen*! And, oh, my God, what a fuddy-duddy old poop I am, thinking about that sexual initiation as though it were as marvelous as the Chrysler Building—while the fifteen-year-old daughter of my cook is taking birth-control pills!

*   *   *

Marilee Kemp said that she was Mr. Gregory's assistant, and that she and he had been deeply moved by my letter. Mr. Gregory, as I might imagine, was a very busy man, and had asked her to reply for him. This was a four-page letter, written in a scrawl almost as childish as my own. She was then only twenty-one years old—the daughter of an illiterate coal miner in West Virginia.

When she was thirty-seven, she would be the Countess Portomaggiori, with a pink palace in Florence, Italy. When she was fifty, she would be the biggest Sony distributor in Europe, and that old continent's greatest collector of American postwar modern art.

*   *   *

My father said she had to be crazy to write such a long letter to a stranger, and nothing but a boy at that, so far away.

Mother said she must be very lonely, which was true. Gregory kept her as a pet around the house, because she was so beautiful, and he used her as a model sometimes. But she was certainly no assistant in his business. He had no interest in her opinions about anything.

He never included her in his dinner parties, either, never took her on trips or to a show or out to restaurants or to other people's parties, or introduced her to his famous friends.

*   *   *

Marilee Kemp wrote me seventy-eight letters between 1927 and 1933. I can count them because I still have them, now bound in a hand-tooled leather volume in a slipcase in the library. The binding and slipcase were a gift from dear Edith on our tenth wedding anniversary. Mrs. Berman has found it, as she has found everything of any emotional significance here but the keys to the barn.

She has read all the letters without first asking me if I considered them private, which I surely do. And she has said to me, and this is the first time she has ever sounded awed: "Just one of this woman's letters says more wonderful things about life than every picture in this house. They're the story of a scorned and abused woman discovering that she was a great writer, because that *is* what she became. I hope you know that."

"I know that," I said. It was certainly true: each letter is deeper, more expressive, more confident and self-respecting than the one before.

"How much education did she have?" she asked.

"One year of high school," I said.

Mrs. Berman shook her head in wonder. "What a year that must have been," she said.

* * *

As for my side of the correspondence: my main messages were pictures I had made, which I thought she would show to Dan Gregory, with brief notes attached.

After I told Marilee that Mother had died of tetanus from the cannery, her letters became very motherly, although she was only nine years older than me. And the first of these motherly letters came not from New York City but from Switzerland, where, she said in the letter, she had gone to ski.

Only after I visited her in her palace in Florence after the war did she tell me the truth: Dan Gregory had sent her alone to a clinic there to get rid of the fetus she was carrying.

"I should have thanked Dan for that," she said to me in Florence. "That's when I got interested in foreign languages." She laughed.

* * *

Mrs. Berman has just told me that my cook has had not just one abortion, like Marilee Kemp, but three—and not in Switzerland but in a doctor's office in Southampton. This wearied me, but then, almost everything about the modern world wearies me.

I didn't ask where the cook's carrying Celeste for a full nine months fit in with the abortions. I didn't want to know, but Mrs. Berman gave me the information anyway. "Two abortions before Celeste, and one after," she said.

"The cook told you that?" I said.

"Celeste told me," she said. "She also told me that her mother was thinking of having her tubes tied."

"I'm certainly glad to know all this," I said, "in case of an emergency."

* * *

Back to the past I go again, with the present nipping at my ankles like a rabid fox terrier:

My mother died believing that I had become a protégé of Dan Gregory, from whom I had never heard directly. Before she got sick, she predicted that "Gregorian" would send me to art school, that "Gregorian" would persuade magazines to hire me as an illustrator when I was old enough, that "Gregorian" would introduce me to all his rich friends, who would tell me how I could get rich, too, investing the money I made as an artist in the stock market. In 1928, the stock market never seemed to do anything but go up and up, just like the one we have today! Whoopee!

So she not only missed the stock market crash a year

later, but the realization a couple of years after the crash that I wasn't even indirectly in touch with Dan Gregory, that he probably didn't even know I was alive, that the effusive praise for the artwork I was sending to New York for criticism wasn't coming from the highest paid artist in American history, but from what my father called in Armenian: ". . . maybe his cleaning woman, maybe his cook, maybe his whore."

7

I remember the afternoon I came home from school when I was about fifteen or so, and Father was sitting at the oilcloth-covered table in our little kitchen, with Marilee's letters in a stack before him. He had reread them all.

This was not a violation of my privacy. The letters were family property—if you can call only two people a family. They were like bonds we had accumulated, gilt-edged securities of which I would be the beneficiary when they and I reached maturity. Once they paid off, I would be able to take care of Father, too, and he sure needed help. His savings had been wiped out by the failure of the Luma County Savings and Loan Association, which we and everybody in town had taken to calling "El Banco Busto." There was no federal insurance scheme for bank deposits back then.

El Banco Busto, moreover, had held the mortgage on the little building whose first floor was Father's shop and whose second story was our home. Father used to own the building, thanks to a loan from the bank. After the bank failed, though, its receivers liquidated all its assets, foreclosing all the mortgages which were in arrears, which was most of them. Guess why they were in arrears? Practically everybody had been dumb enough to entrust their savings to El Banco Busto.

So the father I found reading Marilee's letters in the afternoon was a man who had become a mere tenant in a building he used to own. As for the shop downstairs: it was vacant, since he couldn't afford to rent that, too. All his machinery had been sold at auction anyway in order to get a few pennies for what we were: people who had been dumb enough to entrust his or her savings to El Banco Busto.

What a comedy!

*　*　*

Father looked up from Marilee's letters when I came in with my schoolbooks, and he said, "You know what this woman is? She has promised you everything, but she has nothing to give." He named the Armenian sociopath who had swindled him and Mother in Cairo. "She is the new Vartan Mamigonian," he said.

"What do you mean?" I said.

And he said exactly as though the handwritten letters were bonds or insurance policies or whatever: "I have just read the fine print." He went on to say that Marilee's first letters had been rich in phrases like "Mr. Gregory says," and "Mr. Gregory feels," and "Mr. Gregory wants you to know," but that, since the third letter, such locutions had entirely disappeared. "This is a nobody," he said, "who will never be anybody, who is trying to get somebody anyway, by stealing the reputation of Gregorian!"

I felt no shock. Some part of me had noticed the same thing about the letters. Some other part of me had managed to bury the bad, bad implications.

* * *

I asked Father what had triggered this investigation at this time. He indicated ten books which had arrived for me from Marilee soon after I left for school. He had stacked them on the drainboard of our sink, a sink full of dirty dishes and pans. I examined them. They were young people's story classics of the day, *Treasure Island, Robinson Crusoe, The Swiss Family Robinson, The Adventures of Robin Hood and his Merry Men, Tanglewood Tales, Gulliver's Travels, Tales from Shakespeare* and so on. Reading matter for young people before the Second World War was a dozen universes removed from the unwanted pregnancies and incest and minimum-wage slavery and treacherous high school friendships and so on in the novels of Polly Madison.

Marilee had sent me these books because they were vibrantly illustrated by Dan Gregory. They were not only the most beautiful artifacts in our apartment: they were about the most beautiful artifacts in all of Luma County, and I responded to them as such. "How nice of her!" I exclaimed. "Would you look at these! Would you *look* at these?"

"I have," he said.

"Aren't they beautiful?" I said.

"Yes," he said, "they are beautiful. But maybe you can explain to me why Mr. Gregorian, who thinks so highly of you, hasn't signed at least one of them, and perhaps scribbled a little note of encouragement to my gifted son?"

All this was said in Armenian. He never talked anything but Armenian at home after the failure of El Banco Busto.

* * *

Whether the advice and encourgement had come from Gregory or Marilee didn't matter much to me at that point. If I do say so myself, I had become one hell of a good artist for a kid in any case. I was so conceited about my prospects, with or without help from New York City, that I defended Marilee mainly to cheer up Father.

"If this Marilee, whoever she is, whatever she is, thinks so much of your pictures," he said, "why doesn't she sell some of them and send you the money?"

"She's been extremely generous," I replied—and so she had been: generous with her time, but also with the finest artist's materials then available anywhere. I had no idea of their value, and neither did she. She had taken them without permission from the supply room in the basement of Gregory's mansion. I myself would see that room in a couple of years, and there was enough stuff in there to take care of Gregory's needs, as prolific as he was, for a dozen lifetimes. She didn't think he would miss what she sent me, and she didn't ask permission because she was scared to death of him.

He used to hit and kick her a lot.

But about the actual value of the stuff: the paints I was using sure weren't Sateen Dura-Luxe. They were Mussini oils and Horadam watercolors from Germany. My brushes came from Winsor and Newton in England. My pastels and colored pencils and inks came from Lefébvre-Foinet in Paris. My canvas came from Claessen's in Belgium. No other artist west of the Rockies had such priceless art supplies!

For that matter, Dan Gregory was the only illustrator I ever knew who expected his pictures to take their places among the great art treasures of the world, who used materials which might really do what Sateen Dura-Luxe was supposed to do: outlast the smile on the "Mona Lisa." The rest of them were satisfied if their work survived the trip to the print shop. They commonly sneered that they did such hack work only for money, that it was art for people who didn't know anything about art—but not Dan Gregory.

* * *

"She is *using* you," said my father.

"For what?" I said.

"So she can feel like a big shot," he said.

* * *

The widow Berman agrees that Marilee *was* using me, but not in the way my father thought. "You were her *audience*," she said. "Writers will *kill* for an audience."

"An audience of *one*?" I said.

"That's all she needed," she said. "That's all anybody needs. Just look at how her handwriting improved and her vocabulary grew. Look at all the things she found to talk about, as soon as she realized you were hanging on every word. She certainly couldn't write for that bastard Gregory. There was no point in writing to the folks back home, either. They couldn't even read! Did you really believe her when she said she was describing things she saw around the city because you might want to paint pictures of them?"

"Yes—" I said, "I guess I did." Marilee wrote long descriptions of breadlines for all the people who had been put out of work by the Depression, and of men in nice suits who obviously used to have money, but who were now selling apples on street corners, and of a legless man on a sort of skateboard, who was a World War One veteran or was pretending to be one, selling pencils in Grand Central Station, and of high-society people thrilled to be hobnobbing with gangsters in speakeasies—that sort of thing.

"That's the secret of how to enjoy writing and how to make yourself meet high standards," said Mrs. Berman. "You don't write for the whole world, and you don't write for ten people, or two. You write for just one person."

* * *

"Who's the one person *you* write for?" I asked.

And she said, "This is going to sound very strange, because you'd think it would be somebody the same age as my readers, but it isn't. That's the secret ingredient of my books, I think. That's why they seem so strong and trustworthy to young people, why I don't sound like one dumb teenager talking to another one. I don't put anything down on paper which Abe Berman wouldn't find interesting and truthful."

Abe Berman, of course, was her brain surgeon husband who died of a stroke seven months ago.

* * *

She has asked me for the keys to the barn again. I told her if she ever even *mentioned* the barn again, I was going to tell everybody that she was really Polly Madison—invite the local papers to come on over and interview her, and so on. If I actually did that, it would not only wreck Paul Slazinger: it would also attract a lynch mob of religious fundamentalists to our doorstep.

I happened to watch the sermon of a television evangelist the other night, and he said Satan was making a four-pronged attack on the American family with communism, drugs, rock and roll, and books by Satan's sister, who was Polly Madison.

* * *

To return to my correspondence with Marilee Kemp: My notes to her cooled after father denounced her as the new Vartan Mamigonian. I was no longer counting on her for anything. Simply as part of the growing-up process, I didn't want her to go on trying to be my substitute mother. I was becoming a man, and didn't need a mother anymore, or so I thought.

Without any help from her, in fact, I had started to make money as an artist, as young as I was, and right there in bankrupt little San Ignacio. I had gone to the local paper, the *Luma County Clarion,* looking for work of any kind after school, and had mentioned that I could draw pretty well. The editor asked me if I could draw a picture of the Italian dictator Benito Mussolini, Dan Gregory's hero of heroes, incidentally, and I did so in two or three minutes maybe, without having to refer to a photograph.

Then he had me draw a beautiful female angel, and I did that.

Then he had me draw a picture of Mussolini pouring a quart of something into the mouth of the angel. He had me label the bottle CASTOR OIL and the angel WORLD PEACE. Mussolini liked to punish people by making them drink a quart of castor oil. That sounded like a comical way to teach somebody a lesson, but it wasn't. The victims often vomited and shit themselves to death. Those who survived were all torn up inside.

That is how I became a paid political cartoonist at a tender age. I did one cartoon a week, with the editor telling me exactly what to draw.

* * *

Much to my surprise, Father began to blossom as an artist, too. In all the guessing about where my artistic talent might have come from, one thing seemed certain: it hadn't come from him or from anybody on his side of the family. When he still had his shoe repair shop, I never saw him do anything imaginative with all the scraps lying around, maybe make a fancy belt for me or a purse for Mother. He was a no-nonsense repairman, and that was all.

But then, as though he were in a trance, and using the simplest hand-tools, he began to make perfectly beautiful cowboy boots, which he sold from door to door. They weren't only tough and comfortable: they were dazzling jewelry for manly feet and calves, scintillating with gold and silver stars and eagles and flowers and bucking broncos cut from flattened tin cans and bottle caps.

But this new development in his life wasn't as nice for me to see as you might think.

It gave me the creeps, actually, because I would look into his eyes, and there wasn't anybody home anymore.

* * *

I would see the same thing happen to Terry Kitchen years later. He used to be my closest friend. And suddenly he began to paint the pictures which make many people say today that he was the greatest of all the Abstract Expressionists—superior to Pollock, to Rothko.

That was fine, I guess, except that when I looked into my best friend's eyes, there wasn't anybody home anymore.

* * *

Ah, me.

Anyway: back around Christmas in 1932, Marilee's most recent letters were lying around somewhere, mostly unread. I had become bored with being her audience.

And then this telegram arrived, addressed to me.

Father would comment before we opened it that it was the first telegram our family had ever received.

The message was this:

BE MY APPRENTICE. WILL PAY
TRANSPORTATION HERE PLUS FREE ROOM,
BOARD, MODEST ALLOWANCE, ART LESSONS.
                                DAN GREGORY.

8

The first person I told about this magnificent opportunity was the old newspaper editor for whom I had been drawing cartoons. His name was Arnold Coates, and he said this to me:

"You really are an artist, and you have to get out of here or you'll shrivel up like a raisin. Don't worry about your father. He's a perfectly contented, self-sufficient zombie, if you'll pardon my saying so.

"New York is just going to be a stopover for you," he went on. "Europe is where the real painters are, and always will be."

He was wrong about that.

"I never prayed before, but I'll pray tonight that you never go to Europe as a soldier. We should never get suckered again into providing meat for the cannons and machine guns they love so much. They could go to war at any time. Look how big their armies are in the midst of a Great Depression!

"If the cities are still standing when you get to Europe," he said, "and you sit in a café for hours, sipping coffee or wine or beer, and discussing painting and music and literature, just remember that the Europeans around you, who you think are so much more civilized than Americans, are looking forward to just one thing: the time when it will become legal to kill each other and knock everything down again.

"If I had my way," he said, "American geography books would call those European countries by their right names: 'The Syphilis Empire,' 'The Republic of Suicide,' 'Dementia Praecox,' which of course borders on beautiful 'Paranoia.'

"There!" he said. "I've spoiled Europe for you, and you haven't even seen it yet. And maybe I've spoiled art for you, too, but I hope not. I don't see how artists can be blamed if their beautiful and usually innocent creations for some reason just make Europeans unhappier and more bloodthirsty all the time."

* * *

That was an ordinary way for a patriotic American to talk back then. It's hard to believe how sick of war we used to be. We used to boast of how small our Army and Navy were, and how little influence generals and admirals had in Washington. We used to call armaments manufacturers "Merchants of Death."

Can you imagine that?

* * *

Nowadays, of course, just about our only solvent industry is the merchandising of death, bankrolled by our grandchildren, so that the message of our principal art forms, movies and television and political speeches and newspaper columns, for the sake of the economy, simply *has* to be this: War is hell, all right, but the only way a boy can become a man is in a shoot-out of some kind, preferably, but by no means necessarily, on a battlefield.

* * *

So I went to New York City to be born again.

It was and remains easy for most Americans to go somewhere else to start anew. I wasn't like my parents. I didn't have any supposedly sacred piece of land or shoals of friends and relatives to leave behind. Nowhere has the number *zero* been more of philosophical value than in the United States.

"Here goes nothing," says the American as he goes off the high diving board.

Yes, and my mind really was as blank as an embryo's as I crossed this great continent on womblike Pullman cars. It was as though there had never been a San Ignacio. Yes, and when the Twentieth Century Limited from Chicago plunged into a tunnel under New York City, with its lining of pipes and wires, I was out of the womb and into the birth canal.

Ten minutes later I was born in Grand Central Station, wearing the first suit I had ever owned, and carrying a cardboard valise and a portfolio of my very best drawings.

Who was there to welcome this beguiling Armenian infant?

Not a soul, not a soul.

* * *

I would have made a great Dan Gregory illustration for a story about a yokel finding himself all alone in a big city he has never seen before. I had got my suit through the mail from Sears, Roebuck, and nobody could draw cheap, mail-order clothes like Dan Gregory. My shoes were old and cracked, but I had shined them and put new rubber heels on them myself. I had also threaded in new laces, but one of those had broken somewhere around Kansas City. A truly observant person would have noticed the clumsy splice in the broken shoelaces. Nobody could describe the economic and spiritual condition of a character in terms of his shoes like Dan Gregory.

My face, however, was wrong for a yokel in a magazine story back then. Gregory would have had to make me an Anglo-Saxon.

* * *

He could have used my head in a story about Indians. I would have made a passable Hiawatha. He illustrated an expensive edition of *Hiawatha* one time, and the model he used for the title character was the son of a Greek fry cook.

In the movies back then, just about any big-nosed

person whose ancestors came from the shores of the Mediterranean or the Near East, if he could act a little, could play a rampaging Sioux or whatever. The audiences were more than satisfied.

* * *

Now I yearned to get back on the railroad train! I had been so *happy* there! How I adored that train! God Almighty Himself must have been hilarious when human beings so mingled iron and water and fire as to make a railroad train!

Nowadays, of course, everything must be done with plutonium and laser beams.

* * *

And could Dan Gregory ever paint pictures of railroad trains! He used to work from blueprints he got from the manufacturers, so that a misplaced rivet or whatever wouldn't spoil his picture for a railroad man. And if he had done a picture of the Twentieth Century Limited the day I arrived, the stains and dirt on the outside would be native to the run between Chicago and New York. Nobody could paint grime like Dan Gregory.

And where was he now? Where was Marilee? Why hadn't they sent someone to meet me with his great Marmon touring car?

* * *

He knew exactly when I was coming. He was the one who had picked the date, an easy one to remember. It was Saint Valentine's Day. And he had done me so many kindnesses through the mail, and not through Marilee or any flunky. All the messages were in his own handwriting. They were brief, but they were incredibly generous, too. I was not only to buy a warm suit for myself at his expense, but one for Father, too.

His notes were so compassionate! He didn't want me to get scared or make a fool of myself on the trains, so he told me how to act in a Pullman berth and on the dining car, and how much and when to tip the waiters and porters, and how to change trains in Chicago. He couldn't have been nicer to his own son, if he had had a son.

He even went to the trouble of sending me expense money as postal money orders rather than personal checks, which indicated that he knew about the failure of the only bank in San Ignacio.

What I didn't know was that, back in December, when he sent me the telegram, Marilee was in the hospital with both legs and one arm broken. He had given her a shove in his studio which sent her backwards and down the staircase. She looked dead when she hit the bottom, and two servants happened to be standing there—at the bottom of the stairs.

So Gregory was scared and remorseful. When he visited Marilee in the hospital the first time, all shamefaced, he told her he was sorry and loved her so much that he would give her anything she could think to ask for—*anything.*

He probably thought it was going to be diamonds or something like that, but she asked for a human being. She asked for me.

* * *

Circe Berman has just suggested that I was a replacement for the Armenian baby which had been taken from her womb in Switzerland.

Maybe so.

* * *

And then Marilee told Gregory what to say to me in the telegram and then his letters, and how much money to send me for what, and on and on. She was still in the hospital when I reached New York, but she certainly didn't expect him to stand me up at the station.

But that's what he did.

He was turning mean again.

* * *

That wasn't the whole story, either. I wouldn't get the *whole* story until I visited Marilee in Florence after the war. Gregory, incidentally, had been dead and buried in Egypt for about ten years by then.

Only after the war did Marilee, reborn as the Contessa Portomaggiore, tell me that I was the reason she had been pushed down the stairs back in 1932. She had sheltered me from that abashing information, and so, from very different motives, certainly, had Dan Gregory.

But she came up to his studio the night he nearly killed her, to get him to give his serious attention to pictures of mine for the very first time. In all the years I had been sending pictures to New York, he had never looked at one. Marilee thought that this time might be different, since Gregory was happier than she had ever seen him. Why? He had that afternoon received a letter of thanks from the man he believed to be the most brilliant leader on earth, the Italian dictator Mussolini, the man who made his enemies drink castor oil.

Mussolini had thanked him for a portrait of himself which Gregory had painted as a gift. Mussolini was depicted as a general of Alpine troops on a mountaintop at sunrise, and you can bet that every bit of leather and piping and braid and brass and pleating, and all the decorations, were exactly as they should be. Nobody could paint uniforms like Dan Gregory.

Gregory would be shot dead in Egypt eight years later, incidentally, by the British, while wearing an Italian uniform.

* * *

But the point is this: Marilee spread out my pictures on a refectory table in his studio, and he knew what they were. As she had hoped, he ambled over to them with all possible amiability. The moment he looked at them closely, though, he flew into a rage.

But it wasn't the nature of my pictures which infuriated him. It was the quality of the art materials I had used. No boy artist in California could afford such expensive imported colors and paper and canvas. Marilee, obviously, had taken them from his supply room.

So he gave her a shove, and she fell backwards down the stairs.

* * *

Somewhere in here I want to tell about the suit I ordered from Sears, Roebuck along with my own. Father and I measured each other up for the suits, which was strange even in itself, since I can't recall our ever having touched before.

But when the suits arrived, it was obvious that somebody somewhere had misplaced a decimal point where Father's pants were concerned. As short as his legs were, his pants were much shorter. As scrawny as he was around the middle, he couldn't button the pants at the waist. The coat was just perfect, though.

So I said to him, "I'm really sorry about the pants. You'll have to send them back."

And he said, "No. I like it very much. It's a very good funeral suit."

And I said, "What do you mean, 'funeral suit'?" I had this vision of his going to other people's funerals without any pants on—not that he had ever gone to anybody's funeral but my mother's, as far as I know.

And he said, "You don't have to wear pants to your own funeral," he said.

* * *

When I went back to San Ignacio for his funeral five years later, he was laid out in the *coat* of that suit at least, but the bottom half of the casket was closed, so I had to ask the mortician if Father had pants on.

It turned out that he did, and that the pants fit nicely. So Father had gone to the trouble of getting pants that fit from Sears, Roebuck.

But there were two unexpected fillips to the mortician's answer. He wasn't the one who had buried my mother, incidentally. The one who buried my mother had gone bankrupt and left town to seek his fortune elsewhere. The one who was burying my father had come to seek his fortune in San Ignacio, where the streets were paved with gold.

One surprising piece of news from him was that my father was going to be buried wearing a pair of his own cowboy boots, which he had been wearing when he died at the movies.

The other fillip was the undertaker's assumption that Father was a Mohammedan. This was exciting to him. It was his biggest adventure in being uncritically pious in a madly pluralistic democracy.

"Your father is the first Mohammedan I've taken care of," he said. "I hope I haven't done anything wrong so far. There weren't any other Mohammedans to advise me. I would have had to go all the way to Los Angeles."

I didn't want to spoil his good time, so I told him that everything looked perfect to me. "Just don't eat pork too near the casket," I said.

"That's all?" he said.

"That—" I said, "and of course you say 'Praise Allah' when you close the lid."

Which he did.

9

How good were those pictures of mine which Dan Gregory looked at so briefly before he shoved Marilee down the stairs? Technically, if not spiritually, they were pretty darn good for a kid my age —a kid whose self-imposed lessons had consisted of copying, stroke by stroke, illustrations by Dan Gregory.

I was obviously born to draw better than most people, just as the widow Berman and Paul Slazinger were obviously born to tell stories better than most people can. Other people are obviously born to sing and dance or explain the stars in the sky or do magic tricks or be great leaders or athletes, and so on.

I think that could go back to the time when people had to live in small groups of relatives—maybe fifty or a hundred people at the most. And evolution or God or whatever arranged things genetically, to keep the little families going, to cheer them up, so that they could all have somebody to tell stories around the campfire at night, and somebody else to paint pictures on the walls of the caves, and somebody else who wasn't afraid of anything and so on.

That's what I think. And of course a scheme like that doesn't make sense anymore, because simply moderate giftedness has been made worthless by the printing press and radio and television and satellites and all that. A moderately gifted person who would have been a community treasure a thousand years ago has to give up, has to go into some other line of work, since modern communications put him or her into daily competition with nothing but world's champions.

The entire planet can get along nicely now with maybe a dozen champion performers in each area of human giftedness. A moderately gifted person has to keep his or her gifts all bottled up until, in a manner of speaking, he or she gets drunk at a wedding and tap-dances on the coffee table like Fred Astaire or Ginger Rogers. We have a name for him or her. We call him or her an "exhibitionist."

How do we reward such an exhibitionist? We say to him or her the next morning, "Wow! Were you ever *drunk* last night!"

*   *   *

So when I became an apprentice to Dan Gregory, I was going into the ring with the world's champion of commercial art. His illustrations must have made any number of gifted young artists give up on art, thinking, "My God, I could never do anything *that* wonderful."

I was a really cocky kid, I now realize. From the very first, when I began copying Gregory, I was saying to myself, in effect, "If I work hard enough, by golly, *I* can do that, too!"

* * *

So there I was in Grand Central Station, with everybody but me being hugged and kissed by everybody, seemingly. I had doubted that Dan Gregory would come to greet me, but where was Marilee?

Did she know what I looked like? Of course. I had sent her many self-portraits, and snapshots taken by my mother, too.

Father, by the way, refused to touch a camera, saying that all it caught was dead skin and toenails and hair which people long gone had left behind. I guess he thought photographs were a poor substitute for all the people killed in the massacre.

Even if Marilee hadn't seen those pictures of me, I would have been easy to spot, since I was the darkest passenger by far on any of the Pullman cars. Any passenger much darker than me in those days would have been excluded by custom from Pullman cars—and almost all hotels and theaters and restaurants.

* * *

Was I sure I could spot Marilee at the station? Funnily enough: no. She had sent me nine photographs over the years, which are now bound together with her letters. They were made with the finest equipment by Dan

Gregory himself, who could easily have become a successful photographer. But Gregory had also costumed and posed her each time as a character in some story he was illustrating—the Empress Josephine, an F. Scott Fitzgerald flapper, a cave woman, a pioneer wife, a mermaid, tail and all, and so on. It was and remains hard to believe that these weren't pictures of nine different women.

There were many beauties on the platform, since the Twentieth Century Limited was the most glamorous train of its time. So I locked eyes with woman after woman, hoping to fire the flashbulb of recognition inside her skull. But all I succeeded in doing, I am afraid, was to confirm for each woman that the darker races were indeed leeringly lecherous, being closer than the whiter ones to the gorillas, the chimpanzees.

* * *

Polly Madison, a.k.a. Circe Berman, has just come and gone, having read what is in my typewriter without asking if I minded. I mind a lot!

"I'm in the middle of a sentence," I said.

"Who isn't?" she said. "I just wondered if it wasn't making you feel creepy, writing about people so long ago."

"Not that I've noticed," I said. "I've gotten upset by a lot of things I hadn't thought about for years, but that's about the size of it. Creepy? No."

"Just think about it," she said. "You know about all sorts of terrible things that are going to happen to these people, yourself included. Wouldn't you like to hop into a time machine and go back and warn them, if you could?" She described an eerie scene in the Los Angeles railroad station back in 1933. "An Armenian boy with a cardboard suitcase and a portfolio is saying goodbye to his immigrant father. He is about to seek his fortune in a great city twenty-five hundred miles away. An old man wearing an eye patch, who has just arrived in a time machine from 1987, sidles up. What does the old man say to him?"

"I'd have to think about it," I said. I shook my head. "Nothing. Cancel the time machine."

"Nothing?" she said.

I told her this: "I want him to believe for as long as possible that he is going to become a great painter and a good father."

*　*　*

Only half an hour later: she has popped in and out again. "I just thought of something maybe you could use somewhere," she said. "What made me think of it was what you wrote earlier about how, after your father started making beautiful cowboy boots, you looked into his eyes and there wasn't anybody home anymore—or when your friend Terry Kitchen started painting his best pictures with his spray gun, and you looked into his eyes and there wasn't anybody home anymore."

I gave up. I switched off this electric typewriter. Where did I learn to touch-type? I had taken a course in typing after the war, when I thought I was going to become a businessman.

I sat back in this chair and I closed my eyes. Ironies go right over her head, and especially those relating to privacy, but I tried one anyway. "I'm all *ears*," I said.

"I never told you the very last thing Abe said before he died, did I?" she said.

"Never did," I agreed.

"That was what I was thinking about that first day—when you came down on the beach," she said.

"O.K.," I said.

At the very end, her brain-surgeon husband couldn't talk anymore, but he could still scrawl short messages with his left hand, although he was normally right handed. His left hand was all he had left that still worked a little bit.

According to Circe, this was his ultimate communiqué: "I was a radio repairman."

"Either his damaged brain believed that this was a literal truth," she said, "or he had come to the conclusion that all the brains he had operated on were basically just receivers of signals from someplace else. Do you get the concept?"

"I think I do," I said.

"Just because music comes from a little box we call a radio," she said, and here she came over and rapped me on my pate with her knuckles as though it were a radio, "that doesn't mean there's a symphony orchestra inside."

"What's that got to do with Father and Terry Kitchen?" I said.

"Maybe, when they suddenly started doing something they'd never done before, and their personalities changed, too—" she said, "maybe they had started picking up signals from another station, which had very different ideas about what they should say and do."

* * *

I have since tried out this human-beings-as-nothing-but-radio-receivers theory on Paul Slazinger, and he toyed with it some. "So Green River Cemetery is full of busted radios," he mused, "and the transmitters they were tuned to still go on and on."

"That's the theory," I said.

He said that all he'd been able to receive in his own head for the past twenty years was static and what sounded like weather reports in some foreign language he'd never heard before. He said, too, that toward the end of his marriage to Barbira Mencken, the actress, she acted "as though she was wearing headphones and listening to the *1812 Overture* in stereo. That's when she was becoming a real actress, and not just another pretty girl onstage that everybody liked a lot. She wasn't even 'Barbara' anymore. All of a sudden she was 'Bar-*beer*-ah!'"

He said that the first he heard of the name change was during the divorce proceedings, when her lawyer referred to her as "Barbira," and spelled it for the court stenographer.

Out in the courthouse corridor afterwards, Slazinger asked her: "Whatever happened to Barbara?"

She said Barbara was dead!

So Slazinger said to her: "Then what on Earth did we waste all this money on lawyers for?"

* * *

I said that I had seen the same sort of thing happen to Terry Kitchen the first time he played with a spray rig, shooting bursts of red automobile paint at an old piece of beaverboard he'd leaned against the potato barn. All of a sudden, he, too, was like somebody listening through headphones to a perfectly wonderful radio station I couldn't hear.

Red was the only color he had to play with. We'd gotten two cans of the red paint along with the spray rig, which we'd bought from an automobile repair shop in Montauk a couple of hours before. "Just *look* at it! Just *look* at it!" he'd say, after every burst.

"He'd just about given up on being a painter, and was going into law practice with his father before we got that spray rig," I said.

"Barbira was just about to give up being an actress and have a baby instead," said Slazinger. "And then she got the part of Tennessee Williams's sister in *The Glass Menagerie.*"

*   *   *

Actually, now that I think back: Terry Kitchen went through a radical personality change the moment he saw the spray rig for sale, and not when he fired those first bursts of red at the beaverboard. I happened to spot the rig, and said that it was probably war surplus, since it was identical with rigs I had used in the Army for camouflage.

"Buy it for me," he said.

"What for?" I said.

"Buy it for me," he said again. He had to have it, and he wouldn't even have known what it was if I hadn't told him.

He never had any money, although he was from a very rich old family, and the only money I had was supposed to go for a crib and a youth bed for the house I'd bought in Springs. I was in the process of moving my family, much against their will, from the city to the country.

"Buy it for me," he said again.
And I said, "O.K., take it easy. O.K., O.K."

*   *   *

And now, let us hop into our trusty old time machine, and go back to 1932 again:

Was I angry to be stood up at Grand Central Station? Not a bit. As long as I believed Dan Gregory to be the greatest artist alive, he could do no wrong. And before I was done with him and he with me, I would have to forgive him for a lot worse things than not meeting my train.

*   *   *

What kept him from coming anywhere near to greatness, although no more marvelous technician ever lived? I have thought hard about this, and any answer I give refers to me, too. I was the best technician by far among the Abstract Expressionists, but I never amounted to a hill of beans, either, and couldn't have— and I am not talking about my fiascoes with Sateen Dura-Luxe. I had painted plenty of pictures before Sateen Dura-Luxe, and quite a few afterwards, but they were no damned good.

But let's forget me for the moment, and focus on the works of Gregory. They were truthful about material things, but they lied about time. He celebrated moments, anything from a child's first meeting with a department store Santa Claus to the victory of a gladiator at the Circus Maximus, from the driving of the golden spike which completed a transcontinental railroad to a man's going on his knees to ask a woman to marry him. But he lacked the guts or the wisdom, or maybe just the talent, to indicate somehow that time was liquid, that one moment was no more important than any other, and that all moments quickly run away.

Let me put it another way: Dan Gregory was a taxidermist. He stuffed and mounted and varnished and mothproofed supposedly great moments, all of which turn out to be depressing dust-catchers, like a moosehead bought at a country auction or a sailfish on the wall of a dentist's waiting room.

Clear?

Let me put it yet another way: life, by definition, is never still. Where is it going? From birth to death, with no stops on the way. Even a picture of a bowl of pears on a checkered tablecloth is liquid, if laid on canvas by the brush of a master. Yes, and by some miracle I was surely never able to achieve as a painter, nor was Dan Gregory, but which was achieved by the best of the Abstract Expressionists, in the paintings which have greatness birth and death are always there.

Birth and death were even on that old piece of beaverboard Terry Kitchen sprayed at seeming random so long ago. I don't know how he got them in there, and neither did he.

I sigh. "Ah, me," says old Rabo Karabekian.

10

Back in 1933:

I told a policeman in Grand Central Station Dan Gregory's address. He said it was only eight blocks away, and that I couldn't get lost, since that part of the city was as simple as a checkerboard. The Great Depression was going on, so that the station and the streets teemed with homeless people, just as they do today. The newspapers were full of stories of worker layoffs and farm foreclosures and bank failures, just as they are today. All that has changed, in my opinion, is that, thanks to television, we can *hide* a Great Depression. We may even be hiding a Third World War.

So it was an easy walk, and I soon found myself standing in front of a noble oak door which my new master had used on the cover of the Christmas issue of *Liberty* magazine. The massive iron hinges were rusty. Nobody could counterfeit rust and rust-stained oak like Dan Gregory. The knocker was in the shape of a Gorgon's head, with intertwined asps forming her necklace and hair.

If you looked directly at a Gorgon, supposedly, you were turned to stone. I told that today to the kids around my swimming pool. They had never heard of a Gorgon. I don't think they've heard of anything that wasn't on TV less than a week ago.

* * *

On the *Liberty* cover, as in real life, the lines in the Gorgon's malevolent face and the creases between the writhing asps were infected with verdigris. Nobody could counterfeit verdigris like Dan Gregory. There was a holly wreath around the knocker on the cover, which had been taken down by the time I got there. Some of the leaves had been brown around the edges or spotted. Nobody could counterfeit plant diseases like Dan Gregory.

So I lifted the Gorgon's heavy necklace and let it fall. The *boom* reverberated in an entrance hall whose chandelier and spiral staircase would also be old stuff to me. I had seen them in an illustration of a story about a fabulously rich girl who fell in love with her family's chauffeur: in *Collier's*, I believe.

The face of the man who answered my *boom* was also well known to me, if not his name, since he had been a model for many of Gregory's pictures—including one about a rich girl and her chauffeur. He had been the chauffeur, who in the story would save the girl's father's business after everybody but the girl scorned him as being nothing but a chauffeur. That story, incidentally, was made into the movie *You're Fired*, the second movie to star sound as well as images. The first one was *The Jazz Singer*, starring Al Jolson, who was a friend of Dan Gregory until they had a falling out about Mussolini during my first night there.

The man who opened the door to me had a very good face for an American-style hero, and had in fact been an aviator during the First World War. He was truly Gregory's assistant, what Marilee Kemp had only claimed to be, and would become the only friend who stuck with Gregory to the bitter end. He, too, would be shot while wearing an Italian uniform in Egypt during not his First but his Second World War.

So says this one-eyed Armenian fortune-teller as he peers into his crystal ball.

* * *

"Can I help you?" he said. There wasn't a flicker of recognition in his eyes, although he knew who I was and that I would be coming to the house at any time. He and Gregory had resolved to give me a chilly welcome. I can only guess at their deliberations prior to my arrival, but they must have been along the lines of my being a parasite which Marilee had brought into the house, a thief who had already stolen hundreds of dollars' worth of art materials.

They must have persuaded themselves, too, that Marilee was wholly to blame for her backward somersaults down the studio staircase, and that she had unjustly blamed Gregory. As I say, I myself would believe that until she told me the truth of the matter after the war.

So, just to start somewhere in proving that I was right to be on the doorstep, I asked for Marilee.

"She's in the hospital," he said, still barring the way.

"Oh," I said. "I'm sorry." And I told him my name.

"That's what I figured," he said. But still he wasn't going to ask me in.

So then Gregory, who was about halfway down the spiral staircase, asked him who was at the door, and the man, whose name was Fred Jones, said, as though "apprentice" were another name for tapeworm, "It's your apprentice."

"My what?" said Gregory.

"Your apprentice," said Jones.

And Gregory now addressed a problem I myself had pondered: what was a painter's apprentice supposed to do in modern times, when paints and brushes and so on no longer had to be made right in the painter's workplace?

He said this: "I need an apprentice about as much as I need a squire or a troubadour."

*   *   *

His accent wasn't Armenian or Russian—or American. It was British upper class. If he had so chosen, up there on the spiral staircase, looking at Fred Jones, not at me, he might have sounded like a movie gangster or cowboy, or a German or Irish or Italian or Swedish immigrant, and who knows what else? Nobody could counterfeit more accents from stage, screen and radio than Dan Gregory.

* * *

That was only the *beginning* of the hazing they had planned so lovingly. This was in the late afternoon, and Gregory went back upstairs without greeting me, and Fred Jones took me down into the basement, where I was served a supper of cold leftovers in the servants' dining room off the kitchen.

That room was actually a pleasant one, furnished with early American antiques which Gregory had used in illustrations. I remembered the long table and the corner cupboard full of pewter and the rustic fireplace with a blunderbuss resting on pegs driven into its chimney breast, from a painting he had done of Thanksgiving at Plymouth Colony.

I was put at one end of the table, with my silverware thrown down any which way, and no napkin. I still remember no napkin. While at the other end five places were very nicely set, with linen napkins and crystal and fine china and neatly deployed silverware, and with a candelabrum at their center. The servants were going to have a fine dinner party to which the apprentice was not invited. I was not to consider myself one of them.

Nor did any of the servants speak to me. I might as well have been a bum off the street. Fred Jones moreover stood over me while I ate—like a sullen prison guard.

While I was eating, and more lonesome than I had ever been in my life, a Chinese laundryman, Sam Wu, came in with clean shirts for Gregory. *Pow!* A flash of recognition went off in my skull. I *knew* him! And he must know me! Only days later would I realize why I thought I knew Sam Wu, although he certainly didn't know me. All dressed up in silk robes and wearing a skullcap, this simperingly polite laundryman had been the model for Dan Gregory's pictures of one of the most sinister characters in all of fiction, the Yellow Menace personified, the master criminal Fu Manchu!

*   *   *

Sam Wu would eventually become Dan Gregory's cook, and then go back to being a laundryman again. And he would be the person to whom I sent the paintings I bought in France during the war.

It was a curious and touching relationship we had during the war. I happened to run into Sam in New York City just before I went overseas, and he asked for my address. He had heard on the radio, he said, about how lonesome soldiers could be overseas, and that people should write to them often. He said I was the only soldier he knew well, so he would write to me.

It became a joke in our platoon at mail call. People would say to me things like: "What's the latest news from Chinatown?" or "No letter from Sam Wu this week? Maybe somebody poisoned his chow mein," and so on.

After I got my pictures from him after the war, I never heard from him again. He may not even have liked me much. For him, I was strictly a wartime activity.

*   *   *

Back to 1933:
Since supper was so nasty, I would not have been surprised to be escorted next to a windowless room by

the furnace, and told that that was to be my bedroom. But I was led up three flights of stairs to the most sumptuous chamber any Karabekian had ever occupied, and told to wait there until Gregory had time to see me, which would be in about six hours, at about midnight, Fred Jones estimated. Gregory was giving a dinner party in the dining room right below me for, among others, Al Jolson and the comedian W. C. Fields, and the author whose stories Gregory had illustrated countless times, Booth Tarkington. I would never meet any of them because they would never come back to the house again—after a bitter argument with Gregory about Benito Mussolini.

About this room Jones put me in: It was Dan Gregory's counterfeit, with genuine French antiques, of the bedroom of Napoleon's Empress Josephine. The chamber was a guest room and not Gregory's and Marilee's bedroom. Imprisoning me there for six hours was subtle sadism of a high order indeed. For one thing, Jones, with a perfectly straight face, indicated that this was to be my bedroom during my apprenticeship, as though anybody but a person as lowborn as myself would find it a perfectly ordinary place to sleep. For another: I didn't dare touch anything. Just to be sure I didn't, Jones said to me, "Please be as quiet as possible, and don't touch anything."

One might have thought they were trying to get rid of me.

* * *

I have just given this snap quiz to Celeste and her friends out by the tennis courts: "Identify the following

persons in history: 'W. C. Fields, the Empress Josephine, Booth Tarkington, and Al Jolson.' "

The only one they got was W. C. Fields, whose old
movies are shown on TV.

And I say I never met Fields, but that first night I
tiptoed out of my gilded cage and to the top of the spiral
staircase to listen to the arrival of the famous guests. I
heard the unmistakable bandsaw twang of Fields as he
introduced the woman with him to Gregory with these
words: "This, my child, is Dan Gregory, the love child
of Leonardo da Vinci's sister and a sawed-off Arapahoe."

*   *   *

I complained to Slazinger and Mrs. Berman at supper
last night that the young people of today seemed to be
trying to get through life with as little information as
possible. "They don't even know anything about the
Vietnam War or the Empress Josephine, or what a Gorgon is," I said.

Mrs. Berman defended them. She said that it was a
little late for them to do anything about the Vietnam
War, and that they had more interesting ways of learning about vanity and the power of sex than studying a
woman who had lived in another country one hundred
and seventy-five years ago. "All that anybody needs to
know about a Gorgon," she said, "is that there *is* no such
thing."

Slazinger, who still believes her to be only semiliter-
ate, patronized her most daintily with these words: "As
the philosopher George Santayana said, 'Those who
cannot remember the past are condemned to repeat
it.' "

"Is that a fact?" she said. "Well—I've got news for Mr. Santayana: we're doomed to repeat the past no matter what. That's what it is to be alive. It's pretty dense kids who haven't figured that out by the time they're ten."

"Santayana was a famous philosopher at Harvard," said Slazinger, a Harvard man.

And Mrs. Berman said, "Most kids can't afford to go to Harvard to be misinformed."

*   *   *

I happened to see in *The New York Times* the other day a picture of a French Empire escritoire which was auctioned off to a Kuwaiti for three quarters of a million dollars, and I am almost certain it was in Gregory's guest room back in 1933.

There were two anachronisms in that room, both pictures by Gregory. Over the fireplace was his illustration of the moment in *Robinson Crusoe* when the castaway narrator sees a human footprint on the beach of the island of which he had believed himself to be the sole resident. Over the escritoire was his illustration of the moment when Robin Hood and Little John, strangers who are about to become the best of friends, meet in the middle of a log crossing a stream, each armed with a quarterstaff, and neither one of them willing to back up so that the other one can get to where he would very much like to be.

Robin Hood winds up in the drink, of course.

11

I fell asleep on the floor of that room. I certainly wasn't going to muss the bed or disturb anything. I dreamed I was back on the train, with its *clickety-clack, clickety-clack, ding-ding-ding* and *whoo-ah*. The *ding-ding-ding* wasn't coming from the train, of course, but from signals at crossings, where anybody who didn't give us the right-of-way would be ripped to smithereens. Serve 'em right! They were nothing. We were everything.

A lot of the people who had to stop for us or be killed were farmers and their families, with all their possessions tied every which way on broken-down trucks.

Windstorms or banks had taken away their farms, just as surely as the United States Cavalry had taken the same land from the Indians in their grandfathers' time. The farms that were whisked away by the winds: where are they now? Growing fish food on the floor of the Gulf of Mexico.

These defeated white Indians at the crossings were nothing new to me. I had seen plenty of them passing through San Ignacio, asking the likes of me or my father, or even an emotionally opaque Luma Indian, if we knew of somebody who needed anybody to do work of any kind.

And I was awakened from my railroad dream at midnight by Fred Jones. He said that Mr. Gregory would see me now. He found it unremarkable that I was sleeping on the floor. When I opened my eyes, the tips of his shoes were inches from my nose.

Shoes have played a very important part in the history of the noble Karabekians.

*   *   *

Fred led me to the foot of the staircase down which Marilee had tumbled, which would deliver me up to one end of the holy of holies, the studio. It looked dark up there. I was to climb the stairs alone. It was easy to believe that there was a gallows tree dangling a noose over a trap door up there.

So up I went. I stopped at the head of the stairs, and perceived an impossibility: six free-standing chimneys and fireplaces, with a coal fire glowing in the hearth of every one.

Let me explain architecturally what was really going on. Gregory, you see, had bought three typical New

York brownstones, each one three windows wide, four floors high, and fifty feet deep, with two fireplaces on each floor. I had supposed that he owned only the townhouse with the oak door and the Gorgon knocker infected with verdigris. So I was unprepared for the vista on the top floor, which seemed to violate all laws of time and space by going on and on and on. Down on the lower floors, including the basement, he had joined up to three houses with doors and archways. On the top floor, though, he had ripped out the dividing walls entirely, from end to end and side to side, leaving only those six free-standing fireplaces.

*   *   *

The only illumination that first night came from the six coal fires, and from pale zebra stripes on the ceiling. The stripes were light from a streetlamp below—cut to ribbons by nine windows overlooking East Forty-eighth Street.

Where was Dan Gregory? I could not see him at first. He was motionless and silent—and shapeless in a voluminous black caftan, displaying his back to me, and low, hunched over on a camel saddle before a fireplace in the middle, about twenty feet from me. I identified the objects on the mantelpiece above him before I understood where he was. They were the whitest things in the grotto. They were eight human skulls, an octave arranged in order of size, with a child's at one end and a great-grandfather's at the other—a marimba for cannibals.

There was a kind of music up there, a tedious fugue for pots and pans deployed under a leaking skylight to the right of Gregory. The skylight was under a blanket of melting snow.

*   *   *

"Ker-plunk." Silence. *"Plink-pank."* Silence. *"Ploop."* Silence. That was how the song of the skylight went as my gaze probed Dan Gregory's one indubitable masterpiece, that studio—his one work of breathtaking originality.

A simple inventory of the weapons and tools and idols and icons and hats and helmets and ship models and airplane models and stuffed animals, including a crocodile and an upright polar bear, in the masterpiece would be amazing enough. But think of this: there were fifty-two mirrors of every conceivable period and shape, many of them hung in unexpected places at crazy angles, to multiply even the bewildered observer to infinity. There at the top of the stairs, with Dan Gregory invisible to me, I myself was everywhere!

I know there were fifty-two mirrors because I counted them the next day. Some I was supposed to polish every week. Others I was not to dust on penalty of *death,* according to my master. Nobody could counterfeit images in dusty mirrors like Dan Gregory.

Now he spoke, and rolled his shoulders some, so I could see where he was. And he said this: "I was never welcome anywhere either." He was using his British accent again, which was the only one he ever used, except in fun. He went on: "It was very good for me to be so unwelcome, so unappreciated by my own master, because look what I have become."

*   *   *

He said that his father, the horse trainer, had come close to killing him when he was an infant because his father couldn't stand to hear him cry. "If I started to cry, he did everything he could to make me stop right away," he said. "He was only a child himself, which is easy to forget about a father. How old are you?"

I spoke my first word to him: "Seventeen."

* * *

"My father was only one year older than you are when I was born," said Dan Gregory. "If you start copulating right now, you, too, can have a squalling baby by the time you're eighteen, in a big city like this one—and far from home. You think you're going to set this city on its ear as an artist, do you? Well—my father thought he was going to set Moscow on its ear as a horse trainer, and he found out quickly enough that the horse world there was run by Polacks, and that the highest he was ever going to rise, no matter how good he was, was to the rank of lowest stableboy. He had stolen my mother away from her people and all she knew when she was only sixteen, promising her that they would soon be rich and famous in Moscow."

He stood and faced me. I had not budged from the top of the stairs. The new rubber heels I had put on my old broken shoes were cantilevered in air past the lip of the top step, so reluctant was I to come any farther into this dumbfoundingly complex and mirrored environment.

Gregory himself was only a head and hands now, since his caftan was black. The head said to me, "I was born in a stable like Jesus Christ, and I cried like this:"

From his throat came a harrowing counterfeit of the cries of an unwanted baby who could do nothing but cry and cry.

My hair stood on end.

12

Dan Gregory, or *Gregorian*, as he was known in the Old World, was rescued from his parents when he was about five years old by the wife of an artist named Beskudnikov, who was the engraver of plates for Imperial bonds and paper currency. She did not love him. He was simply a stray, mangy animal in the city she could not stand to see abused. So she did with him what she had done with several stray cats and dogs she had brought home—handed him over to the servants to clean and raise.

"Her servants felt about me the way my servants feel about you," Gregory said to me. "I was just one more

job to do, like shoveling ashes from the stoves or cleaning the lamp chimneys or beating the rugs."

He said he studied what the dogs and cats did to get
along, and then he did that, too. "The animals spent a
lot of time in Beskudnikov's workshop, which was behind his house," he said. "The apprentices and journey-
men would pet them and give them food, so I did that,
too. I did some things the other animals *couldn't* do. I
learned all the languages spoken there. Beskudnikov
himself had studied in England and France, and he
liked to give his helpers orders in one or the other of
those languages, which he expected all of them to understand. Very soon I made myself useful as a translator,
telling them exactly what their master had said to
them. I already knew Polish and Russian, which the
servants had taught me."

"And Armenian," I suggested.

"No," he said. "All I ever learned from my drunken
parents was how to bray like a jackass or gibber like a
monkey—or snarl like a wolf."

He said that he also mastered every craft practiced in
the shop, and, like me, had a knack for catching in a
quick sketch a passable likeness of almost anybody or
anything. "At the age of ten I myself was made an
apprentice," he said.

"By the age of fifteen," he went on, "it was obvious to
everyone that I was a genius. Beskudnikov himself felt
threatened, so he assigned me a task which everyone
agreed was impossible. He would promote me to journeyman only after I had drawn by hand a one-ruble
note, front and back, good enough to fool the sharp-
eyed merchants in the marketplace."

He grinned at me. "The penalty for counterfeiting in

those days," he said, "was a public hanging in that same
marketplace."

*　*　*

Young Dan Gregorian spent six months making what
he and all his co-workers agreed was a perfect note.
Beskudnikov called the effort childish, and tore it into
little pieces.

Gregorian made an even better one, again taking six
months to do so. Beskudnikov declared it to be worse
than the first, and threw it into the fire.

Gregorian made still a better one, spending a full
year on it this time. All the while, of course, he was also
carrying out his regular chores around the shop and
house. When he completed his third counterfeit, however, he put it in his pocket. He showed Beskudnikov
the genuine ruble he had been copying instead.

As he had expected, the old man laughed at that one,
too. But before Beskudnikov could destroy it, young
Gregorian snatched it away and ran out into the marketplace. He bought a box of cigars with the genuine
ruble, telling the tobacconist that the note was *surely*
genuine, since it had come from Beskudnikov, engraver of the plates for the Imperial paper currency.

Beskudnikov was horrified when the boy returned
with the cigars. He had never meant for him to actually
spend his counterfeit in the marketplace. He had
named negotiability simply as his standard for excellence. His bugging eyes and sweaty brow and gasping
proved that he was an honest man whose judgment was
clouded by jealousy. Because his brilliant apprentice
had handed him the ruble, his own work, incidentally,
it really did look like a fake to him.

What could the old man do, now? The tobacconist would surely recognize the note as a fake, too, and know where it had come from. After that? The law was the law. The Imperial engraver and his apprentice would be hanged side by side in the marketplace.

"To his eternal credit," Dan Gregory said to me, "he himself resolved to retrieve what he thought was a fatal piece of paper. He asked me for the ruble I had copied. I of course handed him my perfect counterfeit."

*   *   *

Beskudnikov told the tobacconist a preposterous story about how the ruble his apprentice had spent on cigars had great sentimental value. It was a matter of indifference to the tobacconist, who traded him the real one for the fake.

The old man returned to the workshop beaming. The moment he was inside, however, he promised Gregorian the beating of his life. Until that time, Gregorian had always stood still for his beatings, as a good apprentice should.

This time the boy ran a short distance away and turned to laugh at his master.

"How dare you laugh at a time like this?" cried Beskudnikov.

"I dare to laugh at you now and for the rest of my life," the apprentice replied. He told what he had done with his counterfeit ruble and the real one. "You can teach me no more. I have surpassed you by far," he said. "I am such a genius that I have tricked the engraver of the Imperial currency into passing a counterfeit ruble in the marketplace. My last words on Earth will be a confession to you, should we find ourselves side by side with nooses around our necks in the marketplace. I will say, 'You were right after all. I wasn't as talented as I thought I was. Good-bye, cruel world, good-bye.' "

13

Cocky Dan Gregorian left Beskudnikov's employ that day, and easily became a journeyman under another master engraver and silk screen artist, who made theatrical posters and illustrations for children's books. His counterfeit was never detected, or at any rate was not traced to him or Beskudnikov.

"And Beskudnikov surely never told anyone the true story," he said to me, "of how he and his most promising apprentice came to a parting of the ways."

* * *

He said he had so far done me the favor of making me feel unwelcome. "Since you are so much older than I was when I surpassed Beskudnikov," he went on, "we should waste no time in assigning you work roughly equivalent to copying a ruble by hand." He appeared to consider many possible projects, but I am sure he had settled on the most diabolical one imaginable well before my arrival.

"Aha!" he said. "I've got it! I want you to set up an easel about where you're standing now. You should then paint a picture of this room—*indistinguishable* from a photograph. Does that sound fair? I hope not."

I swallowed hard. "No, sir," I said, "it sure isn't fair." And he said, "Excellent!"

* * *

I have just been to New York City for the first time in two years. It was Circe Berman's idea that I do this, and that I do it alone—so as to prove to myself that I was still a perfectly healthy man, in no way in need of assistance, in no way an invalid. It is now the middle of August. She has been here for two months and a little more, which means that I have been writing this book for two months!

She swore that the city of New York could be a Fountain of Youth for me, if only I would retrace some of the steps I had taken when I first got there from California so long ago. "Your muscles will tell you that they are nearly as springy as they were back then," she said. "If you will only let it," she said, "your brain will show you that it can be exactly as cocky and *excited* as it was back then."

It sounded good. But guess what? She was assembling a booby trap.

            *   *   *

Her promise came true for a little while, not that she gave a damn whether it was hollow or not. All she wanted was to get me out of here for a little while, so she could do what she pleased with this property.

At least she didn't break into the potato barn, which she could have done herself, given enough time—and a crowbar and an axe. She had only to go into the carriage house to find a crowbar and an axe.

            *   *   *

I really did feel spry and cocky again when I retraced my first steps from Grand Central Station to the three brownstones which had been the mansion of Dan Gregory. They were three separate houses again, as I already knew. They had been made separate again about the time my father died, three years before the United States got into the war. Which war? The Peloponnesian War, of course. Doesn't anybody but me remember the Peloponnesian War?

            *   *   *

I begin again:

Dan Gregory's mansion became three separate brownstones again soon after he and Marilee and Fred Jones left for Italy to take part in Mussolini's great social experiment. Although he and Fred were well into their fifties by then, they would ask for and receive permission from Mussolini himself to don Italian infantry officers' uniforms, but without any badges of rank or unit, and to make paintings of the Italian Army in action.

They would be killed almost exactly one year before the United States joined the war—against Italy, by the way, and against Germany and Japan and some others. They were killed around December seventh of 1940 at Sidi Barrani, Egypt, where only thirty thousand British overwhelmed eighty thousand Italians, I learn from the *Encyclopaedia Britannica*, capturing forty thousand Italians and four hundred guns.

When the *Britannica* talks about captured guns, it doesn't mean rifles and pistols. It means great big guns.

Yes, and since Gregory and his sidekick Jones were such weapons nuts, let it be said that it was Matilda tanks, and Stens and Brens and Enfield rifles with fixed bayonets which did them in.

*　*　*

Why did Marilee go to Italy with Gregory and Jones? She was in love with Gregory, and he was in love with her.

How is that for simplicity?

*　*　*

The easternmost house of the three which used to belong to Gregory, I only discovered on this most recent trip to New York, is now the office and dwelling of the Delegation to the United Nations of the Emirate of Salibaar. That was the first I had ever heard of the Emirate of Salibaar, which I can't find anywhere in my *Encyclopaedia Britannica*. I can only find a desert town by that name, population eleven thousand, about the population of San Ignacio. Circe Berman says it is time I got a new encyclopedia, and some new neckties, too.

The big oak door and its massive hinges are unchanged, except that the Gorgon knocker is gone. Gregory took it with him to Italy, and I saw it again on the front door of Marilee's palace in Florence after the war.

Maybe it has now migrated elsewhere, since Italy's and my beloved Contessa Portomaggiore died of natural causes in her sleep in the same week my beloved Edith passed away.

Some *week* for old Rabo Karabekian!

* * *

The middle brownstone has been divided into five apartments, one on each floor, including the basement, as I learned by the mailboxes and doorbells in the foyer.

But don't mention foyers to me! More about that in a little bit! All things in good time!

* * *

That middle house used to contain the guest room where I was first incarcerated, and Gregory's grand dining room right below that, and his research library below that, and the storage room for his art materials in the basement. I was mostly curious, though, about the top floor, which used to be the part of Gregory's studio with the big, leaky skylight. I wanted to know whether there was still a skylight up there, and, if so, if anybody had ever found a way to stop its leaks, or whether there were still pots and pans making John Cage music underneath it when it rained or snowed.

But there was nobody to ask, so I never found out. So

there is one storytelling fizzle for you, dear Reader. I never found out.

And here is another one. The house to the west of that one is, judging from the mailboxes and bells, evidentally a triplex at the bottom, with a duplex on top of that. It was this third of Gregory's establishment which the live-in servants had inhabited, and where I, too, was given a small but cheerful bedroom. Fred Jones's bedroom, by the way, was right in back of Gregory's and Marilee's room in the Emirate of Salibaar.

                    *   *   *

This woman came out of the brownstone with the duplex and triplex. She was old and trembly, but her posture was good, and it was easy to see that she had been very beautiful at one time. I locked my gaze to hers, and a flash of recognition went off in my skull. I knew *her*, but she didn't know *me*. We had never met. I realized that I had seen her in motion pictures when she was much younger. A second later, I came up with her name. She was Barbira Mencken, the ex-wife of Paul Slazinger. He had lost touch with her years ago, had no idea where she lived. She hadn't done a movie or a play for a long, long time, but there she was. Greta Garbo and Katharine Hepburn also live in that same general neighborhood.

I didn't speak to her. Should I have spoken to her? What would I have had to say to her? "Paul is fine and sends his best"? Or how about this one: "Tell me how your parents died"?

                    *   *   *

I had supper at the Century Club, to which I have belonged for many years. There was a new maître d', and I asked him what had happened to the old one, Roberto. He said that Roberto had been killed by a bicycle messenger going the wrong way on a one-way street right in front of the club.

I said that was too bad, and he heartily agreed with me.

I didn't see anybody I knew, which was hardly surprising, since everybody I know is dead. But I made friends in the bar with a man considerably my junior, who was a writer of young adult novels, like Circe Berman. I asked him if he had ever heard of the Polly Madison books and he asked me if I had ever heard of the Atlantic Ocean.

So we had supper together. His wife was out of town lecturing, he said. She was a prominent sexologist.

I asked him as delicately as I could if making love to a woman so sophisticated in sexual techniques was in any way unusually burdensome. He replied, rolling his eyes at the ceiling, that I had certainly hit the nail on the head. "I have to reassure her that I really love her practically *incessantly*," he said.

* * *

I spent an uneventful late evening watching pornographic TV programs in my room at the Algonquin Hotel. I watched and didn't watch at the very same time.

I planned to catch a train back the next afternoon, but met a fellow East Hamptonite, Floyd Pomerantz, at breakfast. He, too, was headed home later in the day, and offered me a ride in his Cadillac stretch limousine. I accepted with alacrity.

What a satisfactory form of transportation that proved to be! That Cadillac was better than womblike. The Twentieth Century Limited, as I have said, really was womblike, in constant motion, with all sorts of unexplained thumps and bangs outside. But the Cadillac was *coffin*like. Pomerantz and I got to be *dead* in there. The hell with this baby stuff. It was so cozy, two of us in a single, roomy, gangster-style casket. Everybody should be buried with somebody else, just about anybody else, whenever feasible.

*　*　*

Pomerantz talked some about picking up the pieces of his life and trying to put them back together again. He is Circe Berman's age, which is forty-three. Three months before, he had been given eleven million dollars to resign as president of a big TV network. "Most of my life still lies ahead of me," he said.

"Yes," I said. "I guess it does."

"Do you think there is still time for me to be a painter?" he said.

"Never too late," I said.

*　*　*

Earlier, I knew, he had asked Paul Slazinger if there was still time for him to become a writer. He thought people might be interested in his side of the story about what happened to him at the network.

Slazinger said afterwards that there ought to be some way to persuade people like Pomerantz, and the Hamptons teem with people like Pomerantz, that they had already extorted more than enough from the economy. He suggested that we build a Money Hall of Fame out here, with busts of the arbitrageurs and hostile-takeover specialists and venture capitalists and investment bankers and golden handshakers and platinum parachutists in niches, with their statistics cut into stone —how many millions they had stolen legally in how short a time.

I asked Slazinger if *I* deserved to be in the Money Hall of Fame. He thought that over, and concluded that I belonged in some sort of Hall of Fame, but that all my money had come as a result of accidents rather than greed.

"You belong in the Dumb *Luck* Hall of Fame," he said. He thought it should be built in Las Vegas or Atlantic City, maybe, but then changed his mind. "The Klondike, I think," he said. "People should have to come by dogsled or on snowshoes if they want to see Rabo Karabekian's bust in the Dumb Luck Hall of Fame."

He can't *stand* it that I inherited a piece of the Cincinnati Bengals, and don't give a damn. He is an avid football fan.

14

So Floyd Pomerantz's chauf-
feur delivered me to the first flagstone of my doorpath.
I clambered out of our fancy casket like Count Dracula,
blinded by the setting sun. I groped my way to my front
door and entered.

Let me tell you about the foyer I had every right to
expect to see. Its walls should have been oyster white,
like every square foot of wall space in the entire house,
except for the basement and servants' quarters. Terry
Kitchen's painting "Secret Window" should have
loomed before me like the City of God. To my left
should have been a Matisse of a woman holding a black

cat in her arms and standing before a brick wall covered with yellow roses, which dear Edith had bought fair and square from a gallery as a present to me on our fifth wedding anniversary. On my right should have been a Hans Hofmann which Terry Kitchen got from Philip Guston in trade for one of his own pictures, and which he gave to me after I paid for a new transmission for his babyshit-brown convertible Buick Roadmaster.

*　*　*

Those who wish to know more about the foyer need only dig out a copy of the February 1981 issue of *Architect & Decorator*. The foyer is on the cover, is viewed through the open front door from the flagstone walk, which was lined on both sides with hollyhocks back then. The lead article is about the whole house as a masterpiece of redecorating a Victorian house to accommodate modern art. Of the foyer itself it says, "The Karabekians' entrance hall alone contains what might serve as the core of a small museum's permanent collection of modern art, marvelous enough in itself, but in fact a mere *hors d'oeuvre* before the incredible feast of art treasures awaiting in the high-ceilinged, stark-white rooms beyond."

And was I, the great Rabo Karabekian, the mastermind behind this happy marriage of the old and the new? No. Dear Edith was. It was all her idea that I bring my collection out of storage. This house, after all, was an heirloom of the Taft family, full not only of memories of Edith's happy childhood in summertimes here, but of her very good first marriage, too. When I moved in here from the potato barn, she asked me if I was comfortable in such old-fashioned surroundings. I said truthfully and from the bottom of my heart that I loved it for what it was, and that she shouldn't change a thing for me.

So by God if it wasn't *Edith* who called in the contractors, and had them strip off all the wallpaper right down to bare plaster, and take down the chandeliers and put up track lights—and paint the oak baseboards and trim and doors and window sashes and walls a solid oyster-white!

When the work was done, she looked about twenty years younger. She said she had almost gone to her grave without ever realizing what a gift she had for remodeling and decorating. And then she said, "Call Home Sweet Home Moving and Storage," in whose warehouse I had stored my collection for years and years. "Let them tell your glorious paintings as they bring them out into the daylight, 'You are going *home*!' "

* * *

When I walked into my foyer after my trip to New York City, though, a scene so shocking enveloped me that, word of honor, I thought an axe murder had happened there. I am not joking! I thought I was looking at blood and gore! It may have taken me as long as a minute to realize what I was really seeing: wallpaper featuring red roses as big as cabbages against a field of black, babyshit-brown baseboards, trim and doors, and six chromos of little girls on swings, with mats of purple velvet, and with gilded frames which must have weighed as much as the limousine which had delivered me to this catastrophe.

Did I yell? They tell me I did. What did I yell? They

had to tell me afterwards what I yelled. They heard it, and I did not. When the cook and her daughter, the first to arrive, came running, I was yelling this, they say, over and over: "I am in the wrong house! I am in the wrong house!"

Think of this: my homecoming was a surprise party they had been looking forward to all day long. Now it was all they could do, despite how generous I had always been with them, not to laugh out loud at my maximum agony!

What a world!

*   *   *

I said to the cook, and I could hear myself now: "Who *did* this?"

"Mrs. Berman," she said. She behaved as though she couldn't imagine what the trouble was.

"How could you allow this to happen?" I said.

"I'm just the cook," she said.

"I also hope you're my *friend*," I said.

"Think what you want," she said. The truth be told, we had never been close. "I like how it looks," she said.

"Do you!" I said.

"Looks better than it did," she said.

So I turned to her daughter. "You think it looks better than it did?"

"Yes," she said.

"Well—" I said, "isn't this just wonderful! The minute I was out of the house, Mrs. Berman called in the painters and paperhangers, did she?"

They shook their heads. They said that Mrs. Berman had done the whole job herself, and that she had met her husband the doctor while papering his office. She used to be a professional paperhanger! Can you beat it?

"After his office," said Celeste, "he had her paper his home."

"He was lucky she didn't paper *him*!" I said.

And Celeste said, "You know you dropped your patch?"

"My what?" I said.

"Your eye patch," she said. "It's on the floor and you're stepping on it."

It was true! I was so upset that at some point, maybe while tearing my hair, I had stripped the patch from my head. So now they were seeing the scar tissue which I had never even shown Edith. My first wife had certainly seen a lot of it, but she was my nurse in the Army hospital at Fort Benjamin Harrison, where a plastic surgeon tried to clean up the mess a little bit after the war. He would have had to do a lot more surgery to get it to the point where it would hold a glass eye, so I chose an eye patch instead.

The patch was on the floor!

* * *

My most secret disfigurement was in plain view of the cook and her daughter! And now Paul Slazinger came into the foyer in time to see it, too.

They were all very cool about what they saw. They didn't recoil in horror or cry out in disgust. It was almost as though I looked just about the same, with or without the eye patch on.

After I got the eye patch back in place, I said to Slazinger: "Were you here while this was going on?"

"Sure," he said. "I wouldn't have missed it for anything."

"Didn't you know how it would make me feel?" I said.

"That's why I wouldn't have missed it for anything," he said.

"I just don't understand this," I said. "Suddenly it sounds as though you're all my enemies."

"I don't know about these two," said Slazinger, "but I'm sure as hell your enemy. Why didn't you tell me she was Polly Madison?"

"How did you find out?" I said.

"She told me," he said. "I saw what she was doing here, and I begged her not to—because I thought it might kill you. She said it would make you ten years younger.

"I thought it might really be a life-and-death situation," he went on, "and that I had better take some direct physical action." This was a man, incidentally, who had won a Silver Star for protecting his comrades on Okinawa by lying down on a fizzing Japanese hand grenade.

"So I gathered up as many rolls of wallpaper as I could," he said, "and ran out into the kitchen and hid them in the deep freeze. How's that for friendship?"

"God *bless* you!" I exclaimed.

"Yes, and God fuck you," he said. "She came right after me, and wanted to know what I'd done with the wallpaper. I called her a crazy witch, and she called me a freeloader and 'the spit-filled penny whistle of American literature.' 'Who are you to talk about literature?' I asked her. So she told me."

What she said to him was this: "My novels sold seven

million copies in the United States alone last year. Two are being made into major motion pictures as we stand here, and one of them made into a movie last year won Academy Awards for Best Cinematography, Best Supporting Actress and Best Score. Shake hands, Buster, with Polly Madison, Literary Middleweight Champion of the World! And then give me back my wallpaper, or I'll break your arms!"

*   *   *

"How could you have let me make such a fool of myself for so long, Rabo—" he said, "giving her tips on the ins and outs of the writing game?"

"I was waiting for the opportune time," I said.

"You missed it by a mile, you son of a bitch," he said.

"She's in a different league from you anyway," I said.

"That's right," he said. "She's richer and she's better."

"Not better, surely," I said.

"This woman is a monster," he said, "but her books are marvelous! She's the new Richard Wagner, one of the most awful people who ever lived."

"How would you know about her books?" I said.

"Celeste has them all, so I read them," he said. "How's that for an irony? There I was all summer, reading her books and admiring the hell out of them, and meanwhile treating her like a half-wit, not knowing who she was."

So that's what *he* did with this summer, anyway: he read all the Polly Madison books!

*   *   *

"After I found out who she was," he said, "and the way you'd kept it from me, I became more enthusiastic than she was about redoing the foyer. I said that if she really wanted to make you happy, she would paint the woodwork babyshit brown."

He knew that I had had at least two unhappy experiences with the color practically everybody calls "babyshit brown." Even in San Ignacio when I was a boy, people called it "babyshit brown."

One experience took place outside Brooks Brothers years ago, where I had bought a summer suit which I thought looked pretty nice, which had been altered for me, and which I decided to wear home. I was then married to Dorothy, and we were still living in the city, and both still planning on my being a businessman. The minute I stepped outside, two policemen grabbed me for hard questioning. Then they let me go with an apology, explaining that a man had just robbed a bank down the street, with a lady's nylon stocking over his head. "All that anybody could tell us about him," one of them said to me, "was that his suit was babyshit brown."

My other unhappy association with that color had to do with Terry Kitchen. After Terry and I and several others in our gang moved out here for the cheap real estate and potato barns, Terry did his afternoon drinking at bars which were, in effect, private clubs for native working men. This was a man, incidentally, who was a graduate of Yale Law School, who had been a clerk to Supreme Court Justice John Harlan, and a major in the Eighty-second Airborne. I was not only supporting him in large measure: I was the one he called or had somebody else call from some bar when he was too drunk to drive home.

And here is what Kitchen, arguably the most important artist ever to paint in the Hamptons, with the possible exception of Winslow Homer, is called in the local bars by the few who still remember him: "The guy in the babyshit-brown convertible."

15

"Where is Mrs. Berman at this moment?" I wished to know.

"Upstairs—getting dressed for a big date," said Celeste. "She looks terrific. Wait till you see."

"Date?" I said. She had never gone on a date as long as she had been living here. "Who would she have a date with?"

"She met a psychiatrist on the beach," said the cook.

"He drives a Ferrari," said her daughter. "He held the ladder for her while she hung the paper. He's taking her to a big dinner party for Jackie Kennedy over in Southampton, and then they're going dancing in Sag Harbor afterwards."

At that moment, Mrs. Berman arrived in the foyer, as serene and majestic as the most beautiful motor ship ever built, the French liner *Normandie*.

* * *

When I was a hack artist in an advertising agency before the war, I had painted a picture of the *Normandie* for a travel poster. And when I was about to sail as a soldier for North Africa on February 9, 1942, and was giving Sam Wu the address where he could write to me, the sky over New York Harbor was thick with smoke.

Why?

Workmen converting an ocean liner into a troopship had started an uncontrollable fire in the belly of the most beautiful motor ship ever built. Her name again, and may her soul rest in peace: the *Normandie*.

* * *

"This is an absolute outrage," I said to Mrs. Berman.

She smiled. "How do I look?" she said. She was overwhelmingly erotic—her voluptuous figure exaggerated and cocked this way and that way as she teetered on high-heeled, golden dancing shoes. Her skintight cocktail dress was cut low in front, shamelessly displaying her luscious orbs. What a sexual bully she could be!

"Who gives a damn what *you* look like?" I said.

"Somebody will," she said.

"What have you *done* to this foyer?" I said. "That's what I'd like to discuss with you, and the *hell* with your clothes!"

"Make it fast," she said. "My date will be here at any time."

"O.K.," I said. "What you have done here is not only

an unforgivable insult to the history of art, but you have spit on the grave of my *wife*! You knew perfectly well that she created this foyer, not I. I could go on to speak of sanity as compared with *in*sanity, decency as compared with vandalism, friendship as compared with rabies. But since you, Mrs. Berman, have called for speed and clarity in my mode of self-expression, because your concupiscent shrink will be arriving in his Ferrari at any moment, try this: Get the hell out of here, and never come back again!"

"Bushwa," she said.

" 'Bushwa'?" I echoed scornfully. "I suppose that's the high level of intellectual discourse one might expect from the author of the Polly Madison books."

"It wouldn't hurt *you* to read one," she said. "They're about life right now." She indicated Slazinger. "You and your ex-pal here never got past the Great Depression and World War Two."

She was wearing a gold wristwatch encrusted with diamonds and rubies which I had never seen before, and it fell to the floor.

The cook's daughter laughed, and I asked her loftily what she thought was funny.

She said, "Everybody's got the dropsies today."

So Circe, picking up the watch, asked who else had dropped something, and Celeste told her about my eye patch.

Slazinger took the opportunity to mock what was under the eye patch. "Oh, you should *see* that scar," he said. "It is the most *horrible* scar! I have never seen such disgusting disfigurement."

I wouldn't have taken that from anybody else, but I had to take it from him. He had a wide scar that looked like a map of the Mississippi Valley running from his sternum to his crotch, where he had been laid open by the hand grenade.

* * *

He has only one nipple left, and he asked me a riddle one time: "What has three eyes, three nipples and two assholes?"

"I give up," I said.

And he said, "Paul Slazinger and Rabo Karabekian."

* * *

There in the foyer, he said to me, "Until you dropped your eye patch, I had no idea how *vain* you were. That's a perfectly acceptable wink under there."

"Now that you know," I said, "I hope that *both* you and Polly Madison clear the hell out of here and never come back again. How you two took advantage of my hospitality!"

"I paid my share," said Mrs. Berman. This was true. From the very first, she had insisted on paying for the cook and the food and liquor.

"You are so deep in my debt for so many things besides money," she went on, "you could never pay me back in a million years. After I'm gone, you're going to realize what a favor I did you with this foyer alone."

"Favor? Did you say *favor*?" I jeered. "You know what these pictures are to anybody with half a grain of sense about art? They are a *negation* of art! They aren't just neutral. They are black holes from which no intelligence or skill can ever escape. Worse than that, they suck up the dignity, the self-respect, of anybody unfortunate enough to have to look at them."

"Seems like a lot for just a few little pictures to do," she said, meanwhile trying without any luck to clip her watch around her wrist again.

"Is it still running?" I said.

"It hasn't run for years," she said.

"Then why do you wear it?" I said.

"To look as nice as possible," she said, "but now the clasp is broken." She offered the watch to me, and made an allusion to my tale of how my mother had become rich in jewels during the massacre. "Here! Take it, and buy yourself a ticket to someplace where you'll be happier—like the Great Depression or World War Two."

I waved the gift away.

"Why not a ticket back to what you were before I got here?" she said. "Except you don't *need* a ticket. You'll be back there quick enough, as soon as I move out."

"I was quite content in June," I said, "and then you appeared."

"Yes," she said, "and you were also fifteen pounds lighter and ten shades paler, and a thousand times more listless, and your personal hygiene was so careless that I almost didn't come to supper. I was afraid I might get leprosy."

"You're *too* kind," I said.

"I brought you back to life," she said. "You're my Lazarus. All Jesus did for Lazarus was bring him back to life. I not only brought you back to life—I got you writing your autobiography."

"That was a big joke, too, I guess," I said.

"Big joke like what?" she said.

"Like this foyer," I said.

"These pictures are twice as serious as yours, if you give them half a chance," she said.

*   *   *

"You had them sent up from Baltimore?" I said.

"No," she said. "I ran into another collector at an antique show in Bridgehampton last week, and she sold them to me. I didn't know what to do with them at first, so I hid them in the basement—behind all the Sateen Dura-Luxe."

"I hope this babyshit brown isn't Sateen Dura-Luxe," I said.

"No," she said. "Only an idiot would use Sateen Dura-Luxe. And you want me to tell you what's great about these pictures?"

"No," I said.

"I've done my best to understand and respect *your* pictures," she said. "Why won't you do the same for *mine*?"

"Do you know the meaning of the word 'kitsch'?" I said.

"I wrote a book called *Kitsch,*" she said.

"I read it," said Celeste. "It's about a girl whose boyfriend tried to make her think she has bad taste, which she does—but it doesn't matter much."

"You don't call these pictures of little girls on swings serious art?" jeered Mrs. Berman. "Try thinking what the Victorians thought when they looked at them, which was how sick or unhappy so many of these happy, innocent little girls would be in just a little while —diphtheria, pneumonia, smallpox, miscarriages, violent husbands, poverty, widowhood, prostitution— death and burial in potter's field."

There was the swish of tires in the gravel driveway. "Time to go," she said. "Maybe you can't stand truly serious art. Maybe you'd better use the back door from now on."

And she was gone!

16

No sooner had the snarl and burble of the psychiatrist's Ferrari died away in the sunset than the cook said she and her daughter would be leaving too. "This is your two weeks' notice," she said.

What a blow! "What made you decide so suddenly?" I asked.

"Nothing sudden about it," she said. "Celeste and I were about to leave right before Mrs. Berman came. It was so *dead* here. She made things exciting, so we stayed. But we've always said to each other: 'When she goes, we go, too.'"

"I really *need* you," I said. "What could I do to persuade you to stay?" I mean: my God—they already had rooms with ocean views, and Celeste's young friends had the run of the property, and no end of free snacks and refreshments. The cook could take any of the cars anytime she wanted to, and I was paying her like a movie star.

"You could learn my name," she said.

What was going on? "Do what?" I said.

"Whenever I hear you talk about me, all you ever call me is 'the cook.' I have a name. It's 'Allison White,' " she said.

"Goodness!" I protested with terrified joviality, "I know that perfectly well. That's who I make out your check to every week. Did I misspell it or something—or get your Social Security wrong?"

"That's the only time you ever think of me," she said, "when you make out my check—and I don't think you think about me then. Before Mrs. Berman came, and Celeste was in school, and there were just the two of us in the house alone, and we'd slept under the same roof night after night, and you ate my food—"

Here she stopped. She hoped she'd said enough, I guess. I now realize that this was very hard for her.

"Yes—?" I said.

"This is so *stupid,*" she said.

"I can't tell if it is or not," I said.

And then she blurted: "I don't want to marry you!"

My God! "Who *would*?" I said.

"I just want to be a human being and not a nobody and a nothing, if I have to live under the same roof with a man—*any* man," she said. She revised that instantly: "Any *person,*" she said.

This was dismayingly close to what my first wife Dorothy had said to me: that I often treated her as though I didn't even care what her name was, as though she really weren't there. The next thing the cook said I had also heard from Dorothy:

"I think you're scared to death of women," she said.

"Me, too," said Celeste.

*   *   *

"Celeste—" I said, "you and I have been close, haven't we?"

"That's because you think I'm stupid," said Celeste.

"And she's still too young to be threatening," her mother said.

"So *everybody's* leaving now," I said. "Where's Paul Slazinger?"

"Out the door," said Celeste.

*   *   *

What had I done to deserve this? All I had done was go to New York City for one night, giving the widow Berman time to redecorate the foyer! And now, as I stood in the midst of a life she had ruined, she was off hobnobbing in Southampton with Jackie Kennedy!

"Oh, my," I said at last. "And I know you hate my famous art collection, too."

They brightened some, because, I suppose, I had broached a subject which was a lot easier to discuss than the relationship between women and men.

"I don't hate them," said the cook—said *Allison White, Allison White, Allison White!* This is a perfectly presentable woman, with even features and a trim figure and nice brown hair. I'm the problem. I am not a presentable man.

"They just don't *mean* anything to me," she went on. "I'm sure that's because I'm uneducated. Maybe if I went to college, I would finally realize how wonderful they are. The only one I really liked, you sold."

"Which one was that?" I said. I myself perked up some, hoping to salvage something, at least, from this nightmare: a statement from these unsophisticated people as to which of my paintings, one I had sold, evidently, had had such power that even *they* had liked it.

"The one with the two little black boys and the two little white boys," she said.

I ransacked my mind for any painting in the house which might have been misread in that way by an imaginative and simple person. Which one had two black blobs and two white ones? Again: it sounded a lot like a Rothko.

But then I caught on that she was talking about a painting I had never considered a part of my collection, but simply a souvenir. It was by none other than Dan Gregory! It was a magazine illustration for a Booth Tarkington story about an encounter in the back alley of a middle-western town, not in this century but in the one before, between two white boys and two black—about ten years old.

In the picture, they were obviously wondering if they could be playmates, or whether they had better go their separate ways.

In the story, the two black boys had very comical names: "Herman" and "Verman." I often heard it said that nobody could paint black people like Dan Gregory, but he did it entirely from photographs. One of the first things he ever said to me was that he would never have a black person in his house.

I thought that was great. I thought everything he said was great for a little while. I was going to become what *he* was, and regrettably *did* in many ways.

* * *

I sold that painting of the two black boys and the two white boys to a real-estate and insurance millionaire in Lubbock, Texas, who has the most complete collection of Dan Gregory paintings in the world, he told me. As far as I know, he has the *only* such collection, for which he has built a large private museum.

He discovered somehow that I used to be Gregory's apprentice, and he called me up to ask if I had any of my master's works I was willing to part with. I had only that one, which I hadn't looked at for years, since it hung in the bathroom of one of the many guest rooms here which I had had no reason to enter.

"You sold the only picture that was really about something," said Allison White. "I used to look at it and try and guess what would happen next."

* * *

Oh: one last thing Allison White said to me before she and Celeste went upstairs to their quarters which had priceless ocean views: "We'll get out of your way now," she said, "and we don't care if we never find out what's in the potato barn."

* * *

So there I was all alone downstairs. I was afraid to go upstairs. I didn't want to be in the house at all, and seriously considered taking up residence again as what I had been to dear Edith after her first husband died: a half-tamed old raccoon in the potato barn.

So I went walking for hours on the beach—all the way to Sagaponack and back again, reliving my blank-brained, deep-breathing hermit days.

There was a note on the kitchen table from the cook, from *Allison White*, saying my supper was in the oven. So I ate it. My appetite is always good. I had a few drinks, and listened to some music. There was one thing I learned during my eight years as a professional soldier which proved to be very useful in civilian life: how to fall asleep almost anywhere, no matter how bad the news may be.

I was awakened at two in the morning by someone's rubbing the back of my neck *so* gently. It was Circe Berman.

"Everybody's leaving," I said. "The cook gave notice. In two weeks, she and Celeste will be gone."

"No, no," she said. "I've talked to them, and they're staying."

"Thank God!" I said. "What did you *say* to them? They hate it here."

"I promised them I wasn't leaving," she said, "so they'll stay, too. Why don't you go up to bed now? You'll be very stiff in the morning if you spend all night down here."

"O.K.," I said groggily.

"Mama's been out dancing, but she's home again,"

she said. "Go to bed, Mr. Karabekian. All's well with the world."

"I'll never see Slazinger again," I said.

"What do you care?" she said. "He never liked you and you never liked him. Don't you know *that?*"

17

We made some sort of contract that night. It was as though we had been negotiating its terms for quite some time: she wanted this, I wanted that.

For reasons best known to herself, the widow Berman wants to go on living and writing here rather than return to Baltimore. For reasons all too clear to myself, I am afraid, I want someone as vivid as she is to keep me alive.

What is the biggest concession she has made? She no longer mentions the potato barn.

* * *

To return to the past:

After Dan Gregory at our first meeting ordered me to make a super-realistic painting of his studio, he said that there was a very important sentence he wanted me to learn by heart. This was it: "The Emperor has no clothes."

"Let me hear you say it," he said. "Say it several times."

So I did. "The Emperor has no clothes, the Emperor has no clothes, the Emperor has no clothes."

"That was a really fine performance," he said, "really topping, really first rate." He clapped his hands appreciatively.

How was I supposed to respond to that? I felt like *Alice in Wonderland.*

"I want you to say that out loud and with just that degree of conviction," he said, "anytime anyone has anything good to say about so-called modern art."

"O.K.," I said.

"It's the work of swindlers and lunatics and degenerates," he said, "and the fact that many people are now taking it seriously proves to me that the world has gone mad. I hope you agree."

"I do, I do," I said. It sounded right to me.

"Mussolini thinks so, too," he said. "Do you admire Mussolini as much as I do?"

"Yes, sir," I said.

"You know the first two things Mussolini would do if he took over this country?" he said.

"No, sir," I said.

"He would burn down the Museum of Modern Art and outlaw the word *democracy.* After that he would make up a word for what we really are, make us face up to what we really are and always have been, and then strive for efficiency. Do your job right or drink castor oil!"

About a year later, I got around to asking him what he thought the people of the United States really were, and he said, "Spoiled children, who are begging for a frightening but just Daddy to tell them exactly what to do."

*   *   *

"Draw everything the way it really is," he said.

"Yes, sir," I said.

He pointed to a clipper ship model on a mantelpiece in the murky distance. "That, my boy, is the *Sovereign of the Seas*," he said, "which, using nothing but wind power, was faster than most freighters are today! Think of that!"

"Yes, sir," I said.

"And when you put it into the wonderful picture you are going to paint of this studio, you and I are going to go over your rendering of it with a magnifying glass. Any line in the rigging I care to point to: I expect you to tell me its name and what its function is."

"Yes, sir," I said.

"Pablo Picasso could never do that," he said.

"No, sir," I said.

He removed from a gun rack a Springfield 1906 rifle, then the basic weapon for the United States Infantry. There was an Enfield rifle in there, too, the basic weapon of the British Infantry, a sort of gun which may have killed him. "When you include this perfect killing machine in your picture," he said of the Springfield, "I want it so real that I can load it and shoot a burglar." He pointed to a nubbin near the muzzle and asked me what it was.

"I don't know, sir," I said.

"The bayonet stud," he said. He promised me that he was going to triple or quadruple my vocabulary, starting with the parts of the rifle, each of which had a specific name. We would go from that simple exercise, he said, required of every Army recruit, to the nomenclature of all the bones, sinews, organs, tubes and wires in the human body, required of every student in medical school. This had been required of him as well, he said, during his Moscow apprenticeship.

He asserted that there would be a spiritual lesson for me in my study of the simple rifle and then the bewilderingly complex human body, since it was the human body the rifle was meant to destroy.

"Which represents good and which represents evil—" he asked me, "the rifle or the rubbery, jiggling, giggling bag of bones we call the body?"

I said that the rifle was evil and the body was good.

"But don't you know that this rifle was designed to be used by Americans defending their homes and honor against wicked enemies?" he said.

So I said a lot depended on whose body and whose rifle we were talking about, that either one of them could be good or evil.

"And who renders the final decision on that?" he said.

"God?" I said.

"I mean here on *Earth*," he said.

"I don't know," I said.

"Painters—and storytellers, including poets and playwrights and historians," he said. "They are the justices of the Supreme Court of Good and Evil, of which I am now a member, and to which you may belong some-day!"

How was *that* for delusions of moral grandeur!

Yes, and now that I think about it: maybe the most admirable thing about the Abstract Expressionist paint-ers, since so much senseless bloodshed had been caused by cockeyed history lessons, was their refusal to serve on such a court.

* * *

Dan Gregory kept me around as long as he did, about three years, because I was servile and because he needed company, since he had alienated most of his famous friends with his humorlessness and rage during political arguments. When I said to Gregory that first night that I had heard the famous voice of W. C. Fields from the top of the spiral staircase, he replied that Fields would never be welcome in his house again, and neither would Al Jolson or any of the others who had drunk his liquor and eaten his food that night.

"They simply do not, will not understand!" he said.

"No, sir," I said.

And he changed the subject to Marilee Kemp. He said she was clumsy to begin with, but had gotten drunk on top of that, and had fallen downstairs. I think he honestly believed that by then. He could easily have indicated which stairs she had fallen down, since I was standing right at the top of them. But he didn't. He felt it sufficed to let me know that she had fallen downstairs *somewhere*. What did it matter where?

While he went on talking about Marilee, he never mentioned her name again. She simply became "women." "Women will never take the blame for anything," he said. "No matter what troubles they bring on themselves, they won't rest until they've found some man to blame for it. Right?"

"Right," I said.

"There's only one way they can take anything, and that's *personally*," he said. "You're not even talking about them, don't even know they're in the room, but they will still take anything you say as though it were aimed right at them. Ever notice that?"

"Yes, sir," I said. It seemed that I *had* noticed that, now that he mentioned it.

"Every so often they will get it into their heads that they understand what you're doing better than you do yourself," he said. "You've just got to throw them out, or they will screw up everything! They've got their jobs and we've got ours. We never try to horn in on them, but they'll horn in on us every chance they get. You want some good advice?"

"Yes, sir," I said.

"Never have anything to do with a woman who would rather be a man," he said. "That means she's never going to do what a woman is supposed to do—which leaves you stuck with both what a man's supposed to do and what a woman's supposed to do. You understand what I am saying?"

"Yes, sir, I do," I said.

He said that no woman could succeed in the arts or sciences or politics or industry, since her basic job was to have children and encourage men and take care of the housework. He invited me to test this statement by naming, if I could, ten women who had amounted to anything in any field but domesticity.

I think I could name ten now, but back then all I could come up with was Saint Joan of Arc.

"Jeanne d'Arc," he said, "was a hermaphrodite!"

18

I don't know where this fits into my story, and probably it doesn't fit in at all. It is certainly the most trivial footnote imaginable in a history of Abstract Expressionism, but here it is:

The cook who had begrudgingly fed me my first supper in New York City, and who kept asking, "What next, what next?" died two weeks after I got there. That finally became what was going to happen next: she would drop dead in Turtle Bay Chemists, a drugstore two blocks away.

But here was the thing: the undertaker discovered that she wasn't just a woman, and she wasn't just a man, either. She was somewhat both. She was a hermaphrodite.

An even more trivial footnote: she would be promptly replaced as Dan Gregory's cook by Sam Wu, the laundryman.

* * *

Marilee arrived home from the hospital in a wheelchair two days after my arrival. Dan Gregory did not come down to greet her. I don't think he would have stopped working if the house were on fire. He was like my father making cowboy boots or Terry Kitchen with his spray gun or Jackson Pollock dribbling paint on a canvas on the floor: when he was doing art, the whole rest of the world dropped away.

And I would be like that, too, after the war, and it would wreck my first marriage and my determination to be a good father. I had a very hard time getting the hang of civilian life after the war, and then I discovered something as powerful and irresponsible as shooting up with heroin: if I started laying on just one color of paint to a huge canvas, I could make the whole world drop away.

* * *

And Gregory's total concentration on his work for twelve or more hours a day meant that I, as his apprentice, had a very easy job indeed. He had nothing for me to do, and did not want to waste time inventing tasks. He had told me to make a painting of his studio, but, once he himself got back to work, I think he forgot all about it.

* * *

Did I make a painting of his studio which was virtually indistinguishable from a photograph? Yes, I did, yes I did.

But I was the only person who gave a damn if I even *tried* to work such a miracle, or not. I was so unworthy of his attention, so far from being a genius, a Gregorian to his Beskudnikov, a threat or a son or whatever, that I might as well have been his cook, who had to be told what to prepare for dinner.

Anything! Anything! Roast beef! Paint a picture of this studio! Who cares? Broccoli!

O.K. I would show *him*.

And I did.

* * *

It was up to his real assistant, Fred Jones, the World War One aviator, to think up work for me to do. Fred made me a messenger, which must have been a terrible blow for the messenger service he had been using. Somebody who desperately needed a job, any kind of job, must have been thrown out of work when Fred gave me a handful of subway tokens and a map of New York City.

He also set me the task of cataloguing all the valuable objects in Gregory's studio.

"Won't that bother Mr. Gregory while he's working?" I said.

And he said: "You could saw him off at the waist while singing 'The Star Spangled Banner,' and he wouldn't notice. Just keep away from his eyes and hands."

* * *

So I was up in the studio, just a few feet from Dan Gregory, itemizing in a ledger his extensive collection of bayonets, when Marilee came home. I remember still how full of bad magic all those spearpoints to be put on the ends of rifles seemed to be. One was like a sharpened curtain rod. Another was triangular in cross-section, so that the wound it made wouldn't close up again and keep the blood and guts from falling out. Another one had sawteeth—so it could work its way through bone, I guess. I can remember thinking that war was so horrible that, at last, thank goodness, nobody could ever be fooled by romantic pictures and fiction and history into marching to war again.

Nowadays, of course, you can buy a machine gun with a plastic bayonet for your little kid at the nearest toy boutique.

* * *

The sounds of Marilee's homecoming floated up from down below. I myself, so much in her debt, didn't hurry down to greet her. I think the cook and my first wife were right: I have always been leery of women—possibly because, as Circe Berman suggested at breakfast this morning, I considered my mother faithless, since she had up and died on me.

Maybe so.

Anyway: she had to send for me, and I behaved with formality. I did not know that Gregory had almost killed her because of the art materials she had sent to me. If I had known that, I might still have been very formal. One thing, surely, which prevented my being effusive, was my sense of my own homeliness and powerlessness and virginity. I was unworthy of her, since she was as beautiful as Madeleine Carroll, the most beautiful of all movie stars.

She was cool and stiff with me, too, I have to say, possibly answering formality with formality. There was probably this factor, too: she wanted to make it clear to me, to Fred, to Gregory, to the hermaphrodite cook, to everybody, that she had not caused me to be brought all the way from the West Coast for purposes of hanky-panky.

And if only I could get back there in a time machine, what incredible fortune I could tell for her:

"You will be as beautiful as you are now, but much, much wiser, when you and I are reunited in Florence, Italy, after World War Two. What a war you will have had!

"You and Fred and Gregory will have moved to Italy, and Fred and Gregory will have been killed in the Battle of Sidi Barrani—in Egypt. You will have then won the heart of Mussolini's minister of culture, Bruno, the Oxford-educated Count Portomaggiore, one of Italy's largest landowners. He will also have been head of the British spy apparatus in Italy all through the war."

*   *   *

When I visited her in her palace after the war, incidentally, she showed me a painting given to her by the mayor of Florence. It depicted the death of her late husband before a Fascist firing squad near the end of the war.

The painting was the sort of commercial kitsch Dan

Gregory used to do, and of which I myself was and remain capable.

* * *

Her sense of her place in the world back in 1933, with the Great Depression going on, revealed itself, I think, in a conversation we had about *A Doll's House,* the play by Henrik Ibsen. A new reader's edition of that play had just come out, with illustrations by Dan Gregory, so we both read it and then discussed it afterwards.

Gregory's most compelling illustration showed the very end of the play, with the leading character, Nora, going out the front door of her comfortable house, leaving her middle-class husband and children and servants behind, declaring that she had to discover her own identity out in the real world before she could be a strong mother and wife.

* * *

That is how the play *ends*. Nora isn't going to allow herself to be patronized for being as uninformed and helpless as a child anymore.

And Marilee said to me, "That's where the play *begins* as far as I'm concerned. We never find out how she survived. What kind of job could a woman get back then? Nora didn't have any skills or education. She didn't even have money for food and a place to stay."

* * *

That was precisely Marilee's situation, too, of course. There was nothing waiting for her outside the door of Gregory's very comfortable dwelling except hunger and humiliation, no matter how meanly he might treat her.

A few days later, she told me that she had solved the problem. "That ending is a *fake!*" she said, delighted with herself. "Ibsen just tacked it on so the audience could go home *happy.* He didn't have the nerve to tell what really happened, what the whole rest of the play says *has* to happen."

"What *has* to happen?" I said.

"She has to commit *suicide,*" said Marilee. "And I mean *right* away—in front of a streetcar or something before the curtain comes down. *That's* the play. Nobody's ever seen it, but *that's* the play!"

* * *

I have had quite a few friends commit suicide, but was never able to see the dramatic necessity for it that Marilee saw in Ibsen's play. That I can't see that necessity is probably yet another mark of my shallowness as a participant in a life of serious art.

These are just my *painter* friends who killed themselves, all with considerable artistic successes behind them or soon to come:

Arshile Gorky hanged himself in 1948. Jackson Pollock, while drunk, drove his car into a tree along a deserted road in 1956. That was right before my first wife and kids walked out on me. Three weeks later, Terry Kitchen shot himself through the roof of his mouth with a pistol.

Back when we all lived in New York City, Pollock and Kitchen and I, heavy drinkers all, were known in the Cedar Tavern as the "Three Musketeers."

Trivia question: How many of the Three Musketeers are alive today? Answer: me.

Yes, and Mark Rothko, with enough sleeping pills in his medicine cabinet to kill an elephant, slashed himself to death with a knife in 1970.

What conclusion can I draw from such grisly demonstrations of terminal discontent? Only this: some people are a lot harder than others, with Marilee and me typifying those others, to satisfy.

Marilee said this about Nora in *A Doll's House:* "She should have stayed home and made the best of things."

19

Belief is nearly the whole of the Universe, whether based on truth or not, and I believed back then that sperm, if not ejaculated, was reprocessed by healthy males into substances which made them athletic, merry, brave and creative. Dan Gregory believed this, too, and so did my father, and so did the United States Army and the Boy Scouts of America and Ernest Hemingway. So I cultivated erotic fantasies about making love to Marilee, and behaved as though we were courting sometimes, but only in order to generate more sperm which could be converted into the beneficial chemicals.

I used to shuffle my feet for a long time on a carpet, and then give Marilee an electric shock with my fingertips when she wasn't expecting it—on the back of her neck or her cheek or a hand. How is that for pornography?

I also got her to sneak off with me and do something which would have made Gregory furious, if he had found out about it, which was to go to the Museum of Modern Art.

But she certainly wasn't about to promote me erotically above the rank of pest and playmate. Not only did she love Gregory, but he was also making it very easy for both of us to get through the Great Depression. First things first.

Meanwhile, though, we were innocently exposing ourselves to a master seducer against whose blandishments we were defenseless. It was too late for either of us to turn back by the time we realized how deeply embroiled we had let ourselves become.

Want to guess who or what it was?

It was the Museum of Modern Art.

*   *   *

The theory that sperm, if unspent, was converted into cosmic vitamins seemed validated by my own performances. Running errands for Gregory, I became as cunning as a sewer rat about the fastest ways to get from anywhere to anywhere on the island of Manhattan. I quintupled my vocabulary, learning the names and functions of every important part of every sort of organism and artifact. My most thrilling accomplishment, however, was this: I finished a meticulously accurate painting of Gregory's studio in only six months!

The bone was bone, the fur was fur, the hair was hair, the dust was dust, the soot was soot, the wool was wool, the cotton was cotton, the walnut was walnut, the oak was oak, the horsehide was horsehide, the cowhide was cowhide, the iron was iron, the steel was steel, the old was old and the new was new.

Yes, and the water dripping from the skylight in my painting was not only the wettest water you ever saw: in each droplet, if you looked at it through a magnifying glass, there was the whole damned studio! Not bad! Not bad!

* * *

An idea has just come to me from nowhere, to wit: Might not the ancient and nearly universal belief that sperm could be metabolized into noble actions have been the inspiration for Einstein's very similar formula: "E equals MC squared"?

* * *

"Not bad, not bad," said Dan Gregory of my painting, and I imagined his feeling like Robinson Crusoe on the occasion of Crusoe's understanding that he no longer had his little island all to himself. There was now *me* to reckon with.

But then he said, "However, *not bad* is another term for *disappointing* or worse, wouldn't you say?"

Before I could frame a reply, he had put the picture atop the glowing coals in the fireplace with the skulls on its mantelpiece. Six months' painstaking work went up the flue in a moment.

I managed to ask chokingly, perfectly aghast, "What was the *matter* with it?"

"No *soul*," he said complacently.

So there I was in the thrall of the new Imperial engraver Beskudnikov!

* * *

I knew what he was complaining about, and the com-
plaint wasn't laughable, coming from him. His own pictures were vibrant with the full spectrum of his own
loves, hates and neutralities, as dated as that spectrum
might seem today. If I were to visit that private museum in Lubbock, Texas, where so many of his works
are on permanent display, the pictures would create for
me a sort of hologram of Dan Gregory. I could pass my
hand through it, but it would be Dan Gregory in three
dimensions all the same. He lives!

If I, on the other hand, were to die, God forbid, and if
some magician were to recover every painting of mine,
from the one Gregory incinerated to the last one I will
ever do, and if these were to be hung in a great domed
rotunda so as to concentrate the soul in each one at the
same focal point, and if my own mother and the women
who swore they loved me, which would be Marilee and
Dorothy and Edith, were to stand for hours at that focal
point, along with the best friend I ever had, who was
Terry Kitchen, not one of them would find any reason
to think about me except randomly. There would not
be a trace of their dear departed Rabo Karabekian, or of
spiritual energy of any sort, at the focal point!

What an experiment!

* * *

Oh, I know: I bad-mouthed Gregory's works a while
back, saying he was a taxidermist, and that his pictures

were always about a single moment rather than the flow of life, and so on. But he was sure a better painter than I could ever hope to be. Nobody could put more of the excitement of a single moment into the eyes of stuffed animals, so to speak, than Dan Gregory.

* * *

Circe Berman has just asked me how to tell a good picture from a bad one.

I said that the best answer I had ever heard to that question, although imperfect, came from a painter named Syd Solomon, a man about my age who summers not far from here. I overheard him say it to a very pretty girl at a cocktail party maybe fifteen years ago. She was so wide-eyed and on tippy-toe! She sure wanted to learn all about art from him.

"How can you tell a good painting from a bad one?" he said. This is the son of a Hungarian horse trainer. He has a magnificent handlebar mustache.

"All you have to do, my dear," he said, "is look at a million paintings, and then you can never be mistaken."

It's true! It's true!

* * *

The present again:

I must tell what happened here yesterday afternoon, when I received the first visitors to my collection since the foyer was, to use the decorator's term, "redone." A young man from the State Department escorted three writers from the Soviet Union, one from Tallin, Estonia, where Mrs. Berman's ancestors came from, after the Garden of Eden, of course, and two from Moscow, Dan

Gregory's old hometown. Small world. They spoke no English, but their guide was an able interpreter.

They made no comment on the foyer when they came in, and proved to be sophisticated and appreciative with respect to Abstract Expressionism, quite a contrast with many other guests from the USSR. As they were leaving, though, they had to ask me why I had such trashy pictures in the foyer.

So I gave them Mrs. Berman's lecture on the horrors which awaited these children, bringing them close to tears. They were terribly embarrassed. They apologized effusively for not understanding the true import of the chromos, and said that, now that I had explained them, they were unanimous in agreeing that these were the most important pictures in the house. And then they went from picture to picture, bewailing all the pain each girl would go through. Most of this wasn't translated, but I gathered that they were predicting cancer and war and so on.

I was quite a hit, and was hugged and hugged.

Never before had visitors bid me farewell so ardently! Usually they can hardly think of anything to say.

And they called something to me from the driveway, grinning affectionately and shaking their heads. So I asked the man from the State Department what they had said, and he translated: "No more war, no more war."

20

Back to the past:

When Dan Gregory burned up my painting, why didn't I do to him what he had done to Beskudnikov? Why didn't I mock him and walk out and find a better job? For one thing, I had learned a lot about the commercial art world by then, and knew that artists like me were a dime a dozen and all starving to death.

Consider all I had to lose: a room of my own, three square meals a day, entertaining errands to run all over town, and lots of playtime with the beautiful Marilee.

What a fool I would have been to let self-respect interfere with my happiness!

* * *

After the hermaphroditic cook died, incidentally, Sam Wu, the laundryman, asked for the job and got it. He was a wonderful cook of good, honest American food as well as Chinese delicacies, and Gregory continued to use him as a model for the sinister master criminal Fu Manchu.

* * *

Back to the present:

Circe Berman said to me at lunch today that I ought to try painting again, since it used to give me such pleasure.

My dear wife Edith made the same suggestion one time, and I told Mrs. Berman what I told her: "I have had all I can stand of not taking myself seriously."

She asked me what had been the most pleasing thing about my professional life when I was a full-time painter—having my first one-man show, getting a lot of money for a picture, the comradeship with fellow painters, being praised by a critic, or what?

"We used to talk a lot about that in the old days," I said. "There was general agreement that if we were put into individual capsules with our art materials, and fired out into different parts of outer space, we would still have everything we loved about painting, which was the opportunity to lay on paint."

I asked her in turn what the high point was for writers—getting great reviews, or a terrific advance, or selling a book to the movies, or seeing somebody reading your book, or what?

She said that she, too, could find happiness in a capsule in outer space, provided that she had a finished, proofread manuscript by her in there, along with somebody from her publishing house.

"I don't understand," I said.

"The orgastic moment for me is when I hand a manuscript to my publisher and say, 'Here! I'm all through with it. I never want to see it again,' " she said.

* * *

Back to the past again:

Marilee Kemp wasn't the only one who was trapped like Nora in *A Doll's House* before Nora blew her cork. I was another one. And then I caught on: Fred Jones was still another one. He was so handsome and dignified and honored, seemingly, to be of assistance to the great artist Dan Gregory in any way possible—but he was a Nora, too.

His life had been all downhill since World War One, when he had discovered a gift for flying rattletrap kites which were machine-gun platforms. The first time he got his hands on the joystick of an airplane, he must have felt what Terry Kitchen felt when he gripped a spray gun. He must have felt like Kitchen again when he fired his machine guns up in the wild blue yonder, and saw a plane in front of him draw a helix of smoke and flame—ending in a sunburst far below.

What beauty! So unexpected and pure! So easy to achieve!

Fred Jones told me one time that the smoke trails of falling airplanes and observation balloons were the most beautiful things he ever expected to see. And I now compare his elation over arcs and spirals and splotches in the atmosphere with what Jackson Pollock used to feel as he watched what dribbled paint chose to do when it struck a canvas on his studio floor.

Same sort of happiness!

Except that what Pollock did lacked that greatest of all crowd pleasers, which was human sacrifice.

* * *

But my point about Fred Jones is this: he had found a home in the Air Corps, just as I would find a home in the Corps of Engineers.

And then he was kicked out for the same reason that I was: he had lost an eye somewhere.

So there is something startling I might tell myself as a youth, if I could get back to the Great Depression in a time machine: "Pst—you, the cocky little Armenian kid. Yes, you. You think Fred Jones is funny and sad at the same time? That's what you'll be someday, too: a one-eyed old soldier, afraid of women and with no talent for civilian life."

I used to wonder back then what it was like to have one eye instead of two, and experiment by covering one eye with a hand. The world didn't seem all that diminished when I looked at it with only one eye. Nor do I feel today that having only one eye is a particularly serious handicap.

Circe Berman asked me about being one eyed after we had known each other less than an hour. She will ask anybody anything at any time.

"It's a piece of cake," I said.

* * *

I remember Dan Gregory now, and he really did resemble, as W. C. Fields had said, "a sawed-off Arapahoe," and of Marilee and Fred Jones at his beck and call. I think what great models they would make for a Gregory illustration of a story about a Roman emperor with a couple of blond, blue-eyed Germanic captives in tow.

It is curious that Fred and not Marilee was the captive Gregory liked to parade in public all the time. It was Fred he took to parties and on fox hunts in Virginia and cruises on his yacht, the *Ararat*.

I do not propose to explain this, beyond declaring for a certainty that Gregory and Fred were men's men. They were not homosexuals.

Whatever the explanation, Gregory did not mind at all that Marilee and I took long walks all over Manhattan, with heads snapping around to take second, third, and fourth looks at her. People must have wondered, too, how somebody like me, obviously not a relative, could have won the companionship of a woman that beautiful.

"People think we're in love," I said to her on a walk one day.

And she said, "They're right."

"You know what I mean," I said.

"What do you think love is anyway?" she said.

"I guess I don't know," I said.

"You know the best part—" she said, "walking around like this and feeling good about everything. If you missed the rest of it, I certainly wouldn't cry for you."

So we went to the Museum of Modern Art for maybe the fiftieth time. I had been with Gregory for almost three years then, and was just a shade under twenty years old. I wasn't a budding artist anymore. I was an *employee* of an artist, and lucky to have a job of any kind. An awful lot of people were putting up with any sort of job, and waiting for the Great Depression to end, so that real life could get going again. But we would also have to get through another World War before *real* life could get going again.

Don't you *love* it? This is real life we are now experiencing.

*   *   *

But let me tell you that life seemed as real as Hell back in 1936, when Dan Gregory caught Marilee and me coming out of the Museum of Modern Art.

21

Dan Gregory caught Marilee and me coming out of the Museum of Modern Art while a Saint Patrick's Day parade was blatting and booming northward on Fifth Avenue, a half a block away. The parade caused Gregory's automobile, a convertible Cord, the most beautiful American means of transportation ever manufactured, to be stuck in traffic right in front of the Museum of Modern Art. This was a two-seater with the top down, and with Fred Jones, the old World War One aviator, at the wheel.

What Fred may have been doing with his sperm I never found out. If I had to guess, I would say that he

was saving it up like me. He had that *look* as he sat at
the wheel of that sublime motorcar, but the hell with
Fred. He was going to be O.K. for quite a while longer,
until he was shot dead in Egypt—whereas I was about
to go into the real world, ready or not, and try to stand
on my own two feet!

Everybody was wearing something green! Then as
now, even black people and Orientals and Hasidic Jews
were wearing something green in order not to provoke
arguments with Roman Catholic Irishmen. Marilee and
Dan Gregory and I and Fred Jones were all wearing
green. Back in Gregory's kitchen, Sam Wu was wearing
green.

Gregory pointed a finger at us. He was trembling
with rage. "Caught you!" he shouted. "Stay right there!
I want to *talk* to you!"

He clambered over the car door, pushed his way
through the crowd and planted himself in front of us,
his feet far apart, his hands balled into fists. He had
often hit Marilee, but he had certainly never hit me.
Oddly enough, nobody had ever hit me. Nobody has
ever hit me.

Sex was the cause of our excitement: youth versus
age, wealth and power versus physical attractiveness,
stolen moments of forbidden fun and so on—but Gregory spoke only of gratitude, loyalty and modern art.

As for the pictures in the museum's being genuinely
modern: most of them had been painted before the
First World War, before Marilee and I had been born!
The world back then was very slow to accept changes in
painting styles. Nowadays, of course, *every* novelty is
celebrated immediately as a masterpiece!

* * *

"You parasites! You ingrates! You rotten-spoiled little kids!" seethed Dan Gregory. "Your loving Papa asked just one thing of you as an expression of your loyalty: 'Never go into the Museum of Modern Art.'"

I doubt that many people who heard him even knew that we were in front of a museum. They probably thought he had caught us coming out of a hotel or an apartment house—someplace with beds for lovers. If they took him literally when he called himself a "Papa," they would have had to conclude that he was *my* Papa and not hers, since we looked so much alike.

"It was *symbolic!*" he said. "Don't you understand that? It was a way of proving you were on my side and not theirs. I'm not afraid to have you look at the junk in there. You were part of *my* gang, and proud of it." He was all choked up now, and he shook his head. "That's why I made that very simple, very modest, very easily complied-with request: 'Stay out of the Museum of Modern Art.'"

* * *

Marilee and I were so startled by this confrontation, we may even have gone on holding hands. We had come skipping out and holding hands like Jack and Jill. We probably did go on holding hands—like Jack and Jill.

Only now do I realize that Dan Gregory caught us at a moment when we had somehow agreed that we were going to make love that afternoon. I now think we were out of control, and would have made love whether we had run into him or not. Every time I have told this story before, I have indicated that there would have been no lovemaking if it hadn't been for the confrontation.

Not so.

* * *

"I don't give a *hoot* what pictures you look at," he said. "All I asked was that you not pay your respects to an institution which thinks that the smears and spatters and splotches and daubs and dribbles and vomit of lunatics and degenerates and charlatans are great treasures we should all admire."

Reconstructing what he said to us long ago, I am touched by how careful he and almost all angry males used to be, when in mixed company, not to use words which might offend women and children, such as *shit* and *fuck*.

Circe Berman argues that the inclusion of once-taboo words into ordinary conversations is a good thing, since women and children are now free to discuss their bodies without shame, and so to take care of themselves more intelligently.

I said to her, "Maybe so. But don't you think all this frankness has also caused a collapse of eloquence?" I reminded her of the cook's daughter's habit of referring to anybody she didn't like for whatever reason as "an asshole." I said: "Never did I hear Celeste give a thoughtful explanation of what it was that such a person might have done to earn that proctological sobriquet."

* * *

"Of all the ways to hurt me," Gregory went on in that British accent of his, "you could not have picked a crueler one. I have treated you as a son," he said to me, "and you like a daughter," he said to Marilee, "and this is the thanks I get. And it's not your going in there which is the most insulting. No, it isn't that. It's how *happy* you were when you were coming out! What could that happiness be but a mockery of me and of every person who ever tried to keep control of a paintbrush?"

He said that he was going to have Fred drive him to City Island, where his yacht the *Ararat* was in dry dock, and he was going to live aboard her until Fred could assure him that we were out of his house on Fortyeighth Street, and that every trace of our ever having been there had been removed.

"Out you go!" he said. "Good riddance of bad rubbish!" What a surreal thing this master realist was about to do! He was going to take up residence on an eightyfoot sailing yacht in dry dock! He would have to come and go by ladder, would have to use a boatyard toilet and telephone!

And think of what a bizarre creation his studio was, an hallucination created at tremendous expense and effort!

And he would eventually arrange to have himself and his only friend killed while wearing Italian uniforms!

Everything about Dan Gregory, except for his paintings, had fewer connections with reality and common sense than the most radical modern art!

*   *   *

Bulletin from the present: Circe Berman has just discovered, after questioning me closely, that I have never actually read a whole book by Paul Slazinger, my former best friend.

She, it turns out, has read them all since moving in. I *own* them all. They have a little shelf of honor in the library, and are autographed beneath testimonials as to how close Paul and I have been for so many years. I have read reviews of most of them, and have a pretty good idea of how they go.

I think Paul knew this about me, although we have certainly never discussed it openly. It is impossible for me to take his writings seriously, knowing how reckless he has been in real life. How can I study his published opinions on love and hate and God and man and whether the ends ever justify the means and all that with solemnity? As for a quid pro quo: I don't owe him one. He has never honored me as a painter or collector, nor should he have.

So what was our bond?

Loneliness and wounds from World War Two which were quite grave.

* * *

Circe Berman has broken her silence about the mystery of the locked potato barn. She found a big picture book in the library whose spine is split and whose pages are not only dog eared but splotched with painty fingerprints, although it was published only three years ago. It depicts virtually all the uniforms worn by every sort of regular soldier or sailor or airman during World War Two. She asked me point blank if it had anything to do with what was in the barn.

"Maybe it does and maybe it doesn't," I said.

But I will tell you a secret: it does, it does.

* * *

So Marilee and I slouched home from the Museum of Modern Art like whipped children. We laughed sometimes, too, just fell into each other's arms and laughed and laughed. So we were feeling each other up and liking each other terrifically all the way home.

We stopped to watch a fight between two white men in front of a bar on Third Avenue. Neither one was wearing green. They snarled in some language we did not understand. They may have been Macedonians or Basques or Frisian Islanders, or something like that.

Marilee had a slight limp and a list to the left, as permanent consequences of her having been pushed down the stairs by an Armenian. But another Armenian was groping her and nuzzling her hair and so on, and had an erection with which you might have smashed coconuts. I like to think we were man and wife. Life itself can be sacramental. The supposition was that we would be leaving the Garden of Eden together, and would cleave to one another in the wilderness through thick and thin.

I don't know why we laughed so much.

Our ages again: I was almost twenty, and she was twenty-nine. The man we were about to cuckold or whatever was fifty-three, with only seven more years to go, a mere stripling in retrospect. Imagine having all of seven more years to go!

*   *   *

Maybe Marilee and I laughed so much because we were about to do the one thing other than eat and drink and sleep which our bodies said we were on Earth to do. There was no vengeance or defiance or defilement in it. We did not do it in the bed she and Gregory

shared, or in Fred Jones's bed next door, or in the im-
maculate French Empire guest-room, or in the studio—
and not even on my own bed, although we could have
done it almost anywhere except in the basement, since
Fu Manchu was the only other person in the house just
then. Our brainless lovemaking anticipated Abstract
Expressionism in a way, since it was about absolutely
nothing but itself.

Yes, and I am reminded now of what the painter Jim
Brooks said to me about how he operated, about how all
the Abstract Expressionists operated: "I lay on the first
stroke of color. After that, the canvas has to do at least
half the work." The canvas, if things were going well,
would, after that first stroke, begin suggesting or even
demanding that he do this or that. In Marilee's and my
case, the first stroke was a kiss just inside the front door,
a big, wet, hot, hilariously smeary thing.

Talk about paint!

*   *   *

Marilee's and my canvas, so to speak, called for more
and wetter kisses, and then a groping, goosey, swooning
tango up the spiral staircase and through the grand
dining room. We knocked over a chair, which we set
upright again. The canvas, doing *all* the work and not
just half of it, sent us through the butler's pantry and
into an unused storage room about eight feet square.
The only thing in there was a broken-down sofa which
must have been left by the previous owners. There was
one tiny window, looking northward, into the leafless
treetops of the back garden.

We needed no further instructions from the canvas as

to what to do, should we wish to complete a masterpiece. This we did.

* * *

Nor did I need instructions from the experienced
older woman as to what to do.

Bull's-eye and bull's-eye and bull's-eye again!

And it was so *retroactive!* This was something I had
been doing all my life! It was so *prospective*, too! I would
be doing one hell of a lot of this for the rest of my life.

And so I did. Except that it would never be that good
again.

Never again would the canvas of life, so to speak, help
me and a partner create a sexual masterpiece.

Rabo Karabekian, then, created at least one masterpiece as a lover, which was necessarily created in private and vanished from the Earth even more quickly
than the paintings which made me a footnote in Art
History. Is there nothing I have done which will outlive
me, other than the opprobrium of my first wife and sons
and grandchildren?

Do I care?

Doesn't everybody?

Poor me. Poor practically everybody, with so little
durable good to leave behind!

* * *

After the war, when I told Terry Kitchen something
about my three hours of ideal lovemaking with Marilee,
and how contentedly adrift in the cosmos they made
me feel, he said this: "You were experiencing a *non-
epiphany.*"

"A what?" I said.

"A concept of my own invention," he said. This was back when he was still a talker instead of a painter, long before I bought him the spray rig. As far as that goes, I was nothing but a talker and a painters' groupie. I was still going to become a businessman.

"The trouble with God isn't that He so seldom makes Himself known to us," he went on. "The trouble with God is exactly the opposite: He's holding you and me and everybody else by the scruff of the neck practically *constantly.*"

He said he had just come from an afternoon at the Metropolitan Museum of Art, where so many of the paintings were about God's giving instructions, to Adam and Eve and the Virgin Mary, and various saints in agony and so on. "These moments are very rare, if you can believe the painters—but who was ever nitwit enough to believe a painter?" he said, and he ordered another double Scotch, I'm sure, for which I would pay. "Such moments are often called 'epiphanies' and I'm here to tell you they are as common as houseflies," he said.

"I see," I said. I think Pollock was there listening to all this, although he and Kitchen and I were not yet known as the "Three Musketeers." He was a real painter, so he hardly talked at all. After Terry Kitchen became a real painter, he, too, hardly talked at all.

" 'Contentedly adrift in the cosmos,' were you?" Kitchen said to me. "That is a perfect description of a non-epiphany, that rarest of moments, when God Almighty lets go of the scruff of your neck and lets you be human for a little while. How long did the feeling last?"

"Oh—maybe half an hour," I said.

And he leaned back in his chair and he said with deep satisfaction: "And there you are."

* * *

That could have been the same afternoon I rented studio space for the two of us in a loft owned by a photographer at the top of a building on Union Square. Studio space in Manhattan was dirt cheap back then. An artist could actually afford to live in New York City! Can you imagine that?

After we had rented the studio space, I said to him: "My wife will kill me, if she hears about this."

"Just give her seven epiphanies a week," he said, "and she'll be so grateful that she'll let you get away with anything."

"Easier said than done," I said.

* * *

The same people who believe that Circe Berman's Dolly Madison books are destroying the fabric of American society, telling teenage girls that they can get pregnant if they're not careful and so on, would surely consider Terry Kitchen's concept of non-epiphanies blasphemous. But I can't think of anybody who tried harder than he did to find worthwhile errands to run for God. He could have had brilliant careers in law or business or finance or politics. He was a magnificent pianist, and a great athlete, too. He might have stayed in the Army and soon become a general and maybe Chairman of the Joint Chiefs of Staff.

When I met him, though, he had given all that up in order to be a painter, even though he couldn't draw for sour apples, and had never had an art lesson in his life!

"Something's just got to be worth doing!" he said. "And painting is one of the few things I haven't tried."

* * *

A lot of people, I know, think that Terry could draw realistically, if he wanted to do so. But their only proof of that is a small patch in a painting that used to hang in my foyer here. He never gave the picture a title, but it is now generally known as *Magic Window*.

Except for one little patch, that picture is a typical Kitchen airbrush view of a brightly colored storm system as viewed from an orbiting satellite, or whatever you want to call it. But the little patch, if examined carefully, turns out to be an upside-down copy of John Singer Sargent's full-length "Portrait of Madame X," with her famous milk-white shoulders and ski-jump nose and so on.

I'm sorry, folks: that whimsical insert, that magic window, wasn't Terry's work, and *couldn't* have been Terry's work. It was done at Terry's insistence by a hack illustrator with the unlikely name of Rabo Karabekian.

* * *

Terry Kitchen said that the only moments he ever experienced as non-epiphanies, when God left him alone, were those following sex and the two times he took heroin.

22

Bulletin from the present: Paul Slazinger has gone to Poland, of all places. According to *The New York Times* this morning, he was sent there for a week by the international writers' organization called "PEN"—as a part of a delegation to investigate the plight of his suffocated colleagues there.

Perhaps the Poles will reciprocate, and investigate his plight in turn. Who is more to be pitied, a writer bound and gagged by policemen or one living in perfect freedom who has nothing more to say?

* * *

Bulletin from the present: the widow Berman has installed an old-fashioned pool table dead center in my living room, having sent the furniture it displaced to Home Sweet Home Moving and Storage. This is a real elephant, so heavy that jack posts had to be put in the basement to keep it from winding up down there amid the cans of Sateen Dura-Luxe.

I haven't played this game since my Army days, and never played it very well. But you should see Mrs. Berman clear the table of balls no matter where they are!

"Where did you ever learn to shoot pool like that?" I asked her.

She said that after her father committed suicide she dropped out of high school and, rather than be sexually promiscuous or become an alcoholic in Lackawanna, she spent ten hours a day shooting pool instead.

I don't have to play with her. Nobody has to play with her, and I don't suppose anybody had to play with her in Lackawanna. But a funny thing will happen. She will suddenly lose her deadly accuracy, and have a fit of yawns and will scratch herself as though she had a fit of itching, too. Then she will go up to bed, and sometimes sleep until noon the next day.

She is the moodiest woman I ever knew.

* * *

And what of the broad hints I have given as to the secret of the potato barn? Won't she read them in this manuscript, and easily guess the rest? No.

She keeps her promises, and she promised me when I began to write that, once I reached one hundred and fifty pages, if I ever reached one hundred and fifty pages, she would reward me with perfect privacy in this writing room.

She said further that when I got this far, if I got that far, this book and I would have become so intimate that it would be indecent for her to intrude. And that is nice, I guess, to have earned through hard work certain privileges and marks of respect, except that I have to ask myself: "Who is she to reward or punish me, and what the hell is this: a nursery school or a prison camp?" I don't ask her that, because then she might take away all my privileges.

*　*　*

Two dandified young German businessmen from Frankfurt came to see my wonderful collection yesterday afternoon. They were typical successful post-Nazi entrepreneurs, to whom history was a clean slate. They were so new, new, new. Like Dan Gregory, they spoke English with upper-class British accents, but asked early on if Circe and I understood any German. They wanted to know, it became evident, whether or not they could communicate frankly to each other in that language without being understood. Circe and I said that we did not, although she was fluent in Yiddish, and so understood quite a lot, and so did I, having heard so much of it as a prisoner of war.

We were able to crack their code to this extent: they were only pretending interest in my pictures. They were really after my real estate. They had come seeking signs in me of failing health or intelligence, or domestic or financial distress, which might make it easy for them to diddle me out of my priceless beachfront, where they would be pleased to erect condominiums.

They got precious little satisfaction. After they had departed in their Mercedes coupe, Circe, the child of a Jewish pants manufacturer, said to me, the child of an Armenian shoemaker, *"We* are the Indians now."

* * *

They were West Germans, as I say, but they could just as easily have been fellow citizens of mine from right down the beach. And I wonder now if that isn't a secret ingredient in the attitudes of so many people here, citizens or not: that this is still a virgin continent, and that everybody else is an Indian who does not appreciate its value, or is at least too weak and ignorant to defend himself?

* * *

The darkest secret of this country, I am afraid, is that too many of its citizens imagine that they belong to a much higher civilization somewhere else. That higher civilization doesn't have to be another country. It can be the past instead—the United States as it was before it was spoiled by immigrants and the enfranchisement of the blacks.

This state of mind allows too many of us to lie and cheat and steal from the rest of us, to sell us junk and addictive poisons and corrupting entertainments. What are the rest of us, after all, but sub-human aborigines?

* * *

This state of mind explains a lot of American funeral customs, too. The message of so many obsequies here, if you think about it, is this: that the dead person has

looted this alien continent, and is now returning to his
or her real home with the gold of El Dorado.

* * *

But back to 1936 again! Listen:

Marilee's and my non-epiphany was soon over. We
used it well. Each of us gripped the other's upper arms,
and palpated what there was to palpate there, initiat-
ing, I suppose, an exploration from the very beginning
of what sorts of devices we might be. There was warm,
rubbery stuff over rods of some kind.

But then we heard the big front door open and close
downstairs. As Terry Kitchen once said of a postcoital
experience of his own: "The epiphany came back, and
everybody had to put on their clothes and run around
again like chickens with their heads cut off."

* * *

As Marilee and I were dressing, I whispered to her
that I loved her with all my heart. What else was there
to say?

"You don't. You can't," she said. She was treating me
like a stranger.

"I will be as great an illustrator as he is," I said.

"With some other woman," she said. "Not with me."
Here we had made all this love, but she was acting as
though I were a nobody trying to pick her up in a public
place.

"Did I do something wrong?" I said.

"You didn't do anything right or wrong," she said,
"and neither did I." She stopped dressing to look me
straight in the eyes. I still had two. "This never happened." She resumed the making of her toilette.

"Feel better?" she said.

I told her that I certainly did.

"So do I," she said, "but it won't last long."

Talk about *realism!*

I thought we had made a contract to pair off permanently. Many people used to think that about sexual intercourse. I thought, too, that Marilee might now bear my child. I did not know that she had been rendered sterile by an infection she picked up during an abortion in supposedly germ-free Switzerland. There was so much I didn't know about her, and which I wouldn't find out for fourteen years!

"Where do you think we should go next?" I said.

"Where do I think *who* should go next?" she said.

"Us," I said.

"You mean after we go leave this warm house forever, smiling bravely and holding hands?" she said. "There's an opera for you that'll break your heart."

"Opera?" I said.

"The beautiful, worldly mistress of a great painter twice her age seduces his apprentice, almost young enough to be her son," she said. "They are discovered. They are cast out into the world. She believes that her love and advice will make the boy a great painter, too, and they freeze to death."

That is just about what would have happened, too.

*　*　*

"You have to go, but I have to stay," she said. "I've got a little money saved up—enough to take care of you for a week or two. It's time you got out of here anyway. You were getting much too comfortable."

"How could we ever part after what we just did?" I said.

"The clocks stopped while we did it," she said, "and now they've started up again. It didn't count, so forget it."

"How *could* I?" I said.

"*I* already have," she said. "You're still a little boy, and I need a man to take care of me. Dan is a man."

So I slunk to my room, confused and humiliated. I packed up my belongings. She did not see me out. I had no idea what room she had gone to, or what she might be doing there. Nobody saw me out.

And I left that house forever as the sun went down on Saint Patrick's Day, 1936, without a backward glance at the Gorgon on the front door of Dan Gregory.

* * *

I spent my first night on my own only a block away, at the Vanderbilt YMCA, but would not see or hear from her again for fourteen years. It seemed to me that she had dared me to become a great financial success, and then to come back and take her away from Dan Gregory. I fantasized about that as a real possibility for perhaps a month or two. Such things happened all the time in stories Dan Gregory was given to illustrate.

She would not see me again until I was worthy of her. Dan Gregory was working on a new edition of *Tales of King Arthur and His Knights* when he got rid of me. Marilee had posed as Guinevere. I would bring her the Holy Grail.

* * *

But the Great Depression soon made clear to me that I would never amount to anything. I couldn't even provide decent food and a bed for my worthless self, and was frequently a bum among bums in soup kitchens and shelters for the homeless. I improved myself in libraries while keeping warm, reading histories and novels and poems said to be great—and encyclopedias and dictionaries, and the latest self-help books about how to get ahead in the United States of America, how to learn from failures, how to make strangers like and trust you immediately, how to start your own business, how to sell anybody anything, how to put yourself into the hands of God and stop wasting so much time and precious energy worrying. How to eat right.

I was certainly a child of Dan Gregory, and of the times, too, when I tried to make my vocabulary and familiarity with great issues and events and personalities throughout recorded time equal to those of graduates of great universities. My accent, moreover, was as synthetic as Gregory's, and so, by the way, was Marilee's. Marilee and I, a coal miner's daughter and an Armenian shoemaker's son, remember, had sense enough not to pretend to be upper-class British. We obscured our humble origins in vocal tones and inflections which had no name back then, as nearly as I can remember, but which are now known as "trans-Atlantic"—cultivated, pleasant to the ear, and neither British nor American. Marilee and I were brother and sister in that regard: we sounded the same.

*   *   *

But when I roamed New York City, knowing so much and capable of speaking so nicely, and yet so lonely, and often hungry and cold, I learned the joke at the core of American self-improvement: knowledge was so much junk to be processed one way or another at great universities. The real treasure the great universities offered was a lifelong membership in a respected artificial extended family.

* * *

My parents were born into biological families, and big ones, too, which were respected by Armenians in Turkey. I, born in America far from any other Armenians, save for my parents, eventually became a member of two artificial extended families which were reasonably respectable, although surely not the social equals of Harvard or Yale:

1. The Officer Corps of the United States Army in time of war,
2. the Abstract Expressionist school of painting after the war.

23

I could not get work with any of the companies which had come to know me as Dan Gregory's messenger boy. He had told them, I imagine, although I have no proof of this, that I was self-serving, disloyal, untalented, and so on. True enough. Jobs were so scarce anyway, so why should they give one to anyone as unlike themselves as an Armenian? Let the Armenians take care of their own unemployed.

And it was, in fact, an Armenian who came to my rescue while I was caricaturing willing sitters in Central Park—for the price of a cup of coffee and little more. He was neither a Turkish nor a Russian Armenian, but a

Bulgarian Armenian, whose parents had taken him to Paris, France, in his infancy. He and they had become members of the lively and prosperous Armenian community in that city, then the Art Capital of the World. As I have said, my own parents and I would have become Parisians, too, had we not been diverted to San Ignacio, California, by the criminal Vartan Mamigonian. My savior's original name had been Marktich Kouyoumdjian, subsequently Frenchified to Marc Coulomb.

The Coulombs, then as now, were giants in the tourist industry, with travel agencies all over the world, and orchestrators of tours to almost anywhere. When he struck up a conversation with me in Central Park, Marc Coulomb was only twenty-five, and had been sent from Paris to find an advertising agency to make his family's services better known in the U.S.A. He admired my facility with drawing materials, and said that, if I really wished to become an artist, I would have to come to Paris.

There was an irony lying in wait in the distant future, of course: I would eventually become a member of that small group of painters which would make New York City and not Paris the Art Capital of the World.

Purely on the basis of race prejudice, I think, one Armenian taking care of another, he bought me a suit, a shirt, a necktie, and a new pair of shoes, and took me to the advertising agency he liked best, which was Leidveld and Moore. He told them they could have the Coulomb account if they would hire me as an artist. Which they did.

I never saw or heard from him again. But guess what? On this very morning, as I am thinking about Marc

Coulomb hard for the first time in half a century, *The New York Times* carries his obituary. He was a hero of the French Resistance, they say, and was, at the time of his death, chairman of the board of Coulomb Frères et Cie, the most extensive travel organization in the world.

What a coincidence! But that is all it is. One mustn't take such things too seriously.

*   *   *

Bulletin from the present: Circe Berman has gone mad for dancing. She gets somebody, simply anybody of any age or station, to squire her to every public dance she hears about within thirty miles of here, many of them fund-raisers for volunteer fire departments. The other morning she came home at three in the morning wearing a fire hat.

She is after me to take ballroom dancing lessons being offered at the Elks Lodge in East Quogue.

I said to her: "I am not going to sacrifice my one remaining shred of dignity on the altar of Terpsichore."

*   *   *

I experienced modest prosperity at Leidveld and Moore. It was there that I did my painting of the most beautiful ocean liner in the world, the *Normandie*. In the foreground was the most beautiful automobile in the world, the Cord. In the background was the most beautiful skyscraper in the world, the Chrysler Building. Getting out of the Cord was the most beautiful actress in the world, who was Madeleine Carroll. What a time to be alive!

Improved diet and sleeping conditions did me the

disservice of sending me one evening to the Art Students League with a portfolio under my arm. I wished
to take lessons in how to be a serious painter, and presented myself and my work to a teacher named Nelson
Bauerbeck, a representational painter, as were almost
all of the painting teachers then. He was principally
known as a portraitist, and his work can still be viewed
in at least one place I know of—at New York University,
my old alma mater. He did portraits of two of that
institution's presidents before my time. He made them
immortal, as only paintings can.

*   *   *

There were about twelve students in the room and
busy at their easels, all making pictures of the same
nude model. I looked forward to joining them. They
seemed to be a happy family, and I needed one. I was
not a member of the family at Leidveld and Moore.
There was resentment there about how I'd got my job.

Bauerbeck was old to be teaching—about sixty-five,
I'd guess. I knew from the head of the art department
at the ad agency, who had studied under him, that he
was a native of Cincinnati, Ohio, but had spent most of
his adult life in Europe, as so many American painters
used to do. He was so old that he had conversed, however briefly, with James Whistler and Henry James and
Émile Zola and Paul Cézanne! He also claimed to have
been a friend of Hitler in Vienna, when Hitler was a
starving artist before the First World War.

Old Bauerbeck must have himself been a starving
artist when I met him. Otherwise, he would not have
been teaching at the Art Students League at that ad-

vanced age. I have never been able to find out what
finally became of him. Now you see him, now you don't.

We did not become friends. He leafed through my
portfolio while saying things like this, very quietly,
thank God, so his students could not hear: "Oh, dear,
dear, dear," and "My poor boy," and "Who did this to
you—or did you do it to yourself?"

I asked him what on Earth was wrong, and he said,
"I'm not sure I can put it into words." He really did
have to think hard about it. "This is going to sound very
odd—" he said at last, "but, technically speaking,
there's nothing you can't do. Do you understand what
I'm saying?"

"No," I said.

"I'm not sure I do, either," he said. He screwed up his
face, "I think—I think—it is somehow very useful, and
maybe even essential, for a fine artist to have to somehow make his peace on the canvas with all the things he
cannot do. That is what attracts us to serious paintings, I
think: that shortfall, which we might call 'personality,'
or maybe even 'pain.' "

"I see," I said.

He relaxed. "I think *I* do, too," he said. "It's something I've never had to articulate before. How *interesting!*"

"I can't tell if you've accepted me as a student or
not," I said.

"No, I've rejected you," he said. "It wouldn't be fair
to either one of us if I were to take you on."

I was angry. "You've rejected me on the basis of some
high-flown theory you just made up," I protested.

"Oh, no, no, no," he said. "I rejected you before I
thought of the theory."

"On the basis of what?" I demanded.

"On the basis of the very first picture in your portfolio," he said. "It told me, 'Here is a man without passion.' And I asked myself what I now ask you: 'Why should I teach him the language of painting, since there seems to be absolutely nothing which he is desperate to talk about?' "

* * *

Hard times!

So I signed up for a course in creative writing instead —taught three nights a week at City College by a fairly famous short-story writer named Martin Shoup. His stories were about black people, although he himself was white. Dan Gregory had illustrated at least a couple of them—with the customary delight and sympathy he felt for people he believed to be orangutans.

Shoup said about my writing that I wasn't going to get very far until I became more enthusiastic about describing the looks of things—and particularly people's faces. He knew I could draw, so he found it odd that I wouldn't want to go on and on about the looks of things.

"To anybody who can draw," I said, "the idea of putting the appearance of anything into words is like trying to make a Thanksgiving dinner out of ball bearings and broken glass."

"Then perhaps you had better resign from this course," he said. Which I did.

I have no idea what finally became of Martin Shoup, either. Maybe he got killed in the war. Circe Berman never heard of him. Now you see him, now you don't.

* * *

Bulletin from the present: Paul Slazinger, who himself teaches creative writing from time to time, has come back into our lives in a great big way! All is forgiven, apparently. He is sound asleep here now in an upstairs bedroom. When he wakes up, we shall see what we shall see.

The Rescue Squad of the Springs Volunteer Fire Department brought him here at about midnight last night. He had awakened his neighbors in Springs by yelling for help out different windows of his house—maybe every window he owned before he was through. The Rescue Squad wanted to take him to the Veterans Administration hospital at Riverhead. It was well known that he was a veteran. It is well known that *I* am a veteran.

But he calmed down, and he promised the rescuers that he would be all right if they brought him over here. So they rang my doorbell, and I received them in the foyer with its pictures of little girls on swings. Supported and restrained in the midst of the compassionate volunteers was a straitjacket containing the frantic meat of Slazinger. If I gave them permission, they were going to turn him loose as an experiment.

Circe Berman had come down by then. We were both in our nightclothes. People do strange things when suddenly confronted by a person out of his or her mind. After taking one long, hard look at Slazinger, Circe turned her back on all of us and started straightening the pictures of the little girls on swings. So there was something this seemingly fearless woman was afraid of. She was petrified by insanity.

Insane people are evidently Gorgons to her. If she looks at one, she turns to stone. There must be a story there.

24

Slazinger was a lamb when they unswaddled him. "Just put me to bed," he said. He named the room he wanted to be put in, the one on the second floor with Adolph Gottlieb's "Frozen Sounds Number Seven" over the fireplace and a bay window looking across the dunes to the ocean. He wanted that room and no other, and seemed to feel entitled to sleep there. So he must have been dreaming in detail of moving in with me for hours at least, and maybe even for decades. I was his insurance plan. Sooner or later, he would simply give up, go limp, and have himself delivered to the beach house of a fabulously well-to-do Armenian.

He, incidentally, was from a very old American family. The first Slazinger on this continent was a Hessian grenadier serving as a mercenary with General John Burgoyne, the British general who was defeated by forces commanded in part by the rebel General Benedict Arnold, who would later desert to the British, at the second Battle of Freeman's Farm, north of Albany, two hundred years ago. Slazinger's ancestor was taken prisoner during the battle, and never went home, which was in Wiesbaden, Germany, where he had been the son of—guess what?

A cobbler.

* * *

"All God's chilluns got shoes."
—Old Negro spiritual.

* * *

I would have to say that the widow Berman was a lot scarier than Slazinger the night Slazinger arrived in a straitjacket. He was pretty much the same old Slazinger when the Rescue Squad turned him loose in the foyer. But Circe, almost catatonic, was a Circe I had never seen before.

So I put Slazinger to bed unassisted. I didn't undress him. He didn't have that many clothes on anyway—just Jockey shorts and a T-shirt that said, STOP SHOREHAM. Shoreham is a nuclear generating plant not far away. If it didn't work the way it was supposed to, it might kill hundreds of thousands of people and render Long Island uninhabitable for centuries. A lot of people were opposed to it. A lot of people were for it. I myself think about it as little as possible.

I will say this about it, although I have only seen it in photographs. Never have I contemplated architecture which said more pointedly to one and all: "I am from another planet. I have no way of caring what you are or what you want or what you do. Buster, you have been *colonized.*"

*   *   *

A good subtitle for this book might be this: *Confessions of an Armenian Late Bloomer or Always the Last to Learn.* Listen to this: I never even *suspected* that the widow Berman was a pill freak until the night Slazinger moved in.

After I had put him to bed, with the Belgian linen sheets pulled right up to the nostrils of his big Hessian nose, I thought it might be a good idea to give him a sleeping pill. I didn't have any, but I hoped Mrs. Berman might have some. I had heard her come up the stairs very slowly and go into her bedroom.

Her door was wide open, so I paid her a call. She was sitting on the edge of her bed, staring straight ahead. I asked her for a sleeping pill, and she told me to help myself in the bathroom. I hadn't entered that bathroom since she took up residence. In fact, I don't think I had been in it for years and years. There is a good chance that I had *never* been in that bathroom before.

And, my God—I wish you could see the pills she had! They were apparently samples from drug salesmen which her late doctor husband had accumulated over decades! The medicine cabinet couldn't begin to hold them all! The marble counter-top around the washbasin was about five feet long and two feet wide, I would estimate, and an entire *regiment* of little bottles was deployed there. The scales dropped from my eyes! So much was suddenly *explicable*—the strange salutation when we first met on the beach, the impulsive redecoration of the foyer, the unbeatable pool game, the dancing madness, and on and on.

And which patient needed me most now in the dead of night?

Well—what could I do for a pill freak that she couldn't do better or worse for herself? So I went back to Slazinger empty handed, and we talked about his trip to Poland for a while. Why not? Any port in a storm.

* * *

Here is the solution to the American drug problem suggested a couple of years back by the wife of our President: "Just say no."

* * *

Maybe Mrs. Berman could say no to her pills, but poor Paul Slazinger had no control over the dangerous substances his own body was manufacturing and dumping in his bloodstream. He had no choice but to think all kinds of crazy things. And I listened to him rave on awhile about how well he could write, if only he were in hiding or in prison in Poland, and how the Polly Madison Books were the greatest works of literature since *Don Quixote.*

He did get off one pretty good crack about her, but I don't think it was meant to be a crack, since he was so rapt when he said it. He called her "the Homer of the bubblegum crowd."

And let's just get it out of the way right here and now about the merits of the Polly Madison books. To settle this question in my own mind, without having to actually read them, I have just solicited by telephone the opinions of a bookseller and a librarian in East Hampton, and also the widows of a couple of the old Abstract Expressionist gang who have teenage grandchildren now.

They all said about the same thing, boiling down to this: "Useful, frank, and intelligent, but as literature hardly more than workmanlike."

So there it is. If Paul Slazinger wants to keep out of the nuthouse, it certainly isn't going to help his case if he says he spent this past summer reading all the Polly Madison Books.

* * *

It won't help his case much, either, that when he was a mere stripling he lay face down on a Japanese hand grenade, and has been in and out of laughing academies ever since. He was seemingly born not only with a gift for language, but with a particularly nasty clock which makes him go crazy every three years or so. Beware of gods bearing gifts!

Before he went to sleep the other night, he said that he could not help being what he was, for good or ill, that he was "that sort of molecule."

"Until the Great Atom Smasher comes to get me, Rabo," he said, "this is the kind of molecule I have to be."

* * *

"And what is literature, Rabo," he said, "but an insider's newsletter about affairs relating to molecules, of no

importance to anything in the Universe but a few molecules who have the disease called 'thought.' "

* * *

"It's all so clear to me now," he said. "I understand
everything."

"That's what you said the last time," I reminded him.

"Well—it's clear to me again," he said. "I was put on
Earth with only two missions: to get the Polly Madison
Books the recognition they deserve as great literature,
and to publish my Theory of Revolution."

"O.K.," I said.

"Does that sound crazy?" he said.

"Yes," I said.

"Good," he said. "Two monuments I must build! One
to her and one to me. A thousand years from now her
books will still be read and people will still be discussing
Slazinger's Theory of Revolution."

"That's nice to think about," I said.

He became foxy. "I never *told* you my theory, did I?"
he said.

"No," I said.

He tapped his temple with his fingertips. "That's because I've kept it locked up here all these years in this
potato barn," he said. "You're not the only old man,
Rabo, who has saved the best for last."

"What do you know about the potato barn?" I said.

"Nothing—word of honor: nothing. But why does an
old man lock up anything so tight, so tight, unless he's
saving the best for last?" he said. "It takes a molecule to
know a molecule."

"What's in *my* barn is not the best and is not the
worst, although it wouldn't have to be very good to be

the best I ever did, and it would have to be pretty awful to be the worst," I said. "You want to know what's in there?"

"Sure, if you want to tell me," he said.

"It's the emptiest and yet the fullest of all human messages," I said.

"Which *is*?" he said.

" 'Good-bye,' " I said.

*   *   *

House party!

And who prepares the meals and makes the beds for these increasingly fascinating guests of mine?

The indispensable Allison White! Thank goodness Mrs. Berman talked her into staying!

And while Mrs. Berman, who says she is nine tenths of the way through her latest epic, can be expected to return to Baltimore in the near future, Allison White will not leave me high and dry. For one thing, the stock market crash two weeks ago has reduced the demand for domestic help out this way. For another, she is pregnant again, and determined to carry the fetus to term. So she has *begged* permission to stay on with Celeste for the winter at least, and I have told her: "The more the merrier."

*   *   *

Perhaps I should have scattered milestones along the route this book has taken, saying, "It is now the Fourth of July," and "They say this is the coolest August on record, and may have something to do with the disappearance of ozone over the North Pole," and so on. But

I had no idea that this was going to be a diary as well as an autobiography.

Let me say now that Labor Day was two weeks ago, just like the stock-market crash. So *zingo!* There goes prosperity! And *zingo!* There goes another summertime!

* * *

Celeste and her friends are back in school, and she asked me this morning what I knew about the Universe. She has to write a theme about it.

"Why ask me?" I said.

"You read *The New York Times* every day," she said.

So I told her that the Universe began as an eleven-pound strawberry which exploded at seven minutes past midnight three trillion years ago.

"I'm *serious!*" she said.

"All I can tell you is what I read in *The New York Times*," I said.

* * *

Paul Slazinger has had all his clothes and writing materials brought here. He is working on his first volume of nonfiction, to which he has given this title: *The Only Way to Have a Successful Revolution in Any Field of Human Activity.*

For what it is worth: Slazinger claims to have learned from history that most people cannot open their minds to new ideas unless a mind-opening team with a peculiar membership goes to work on them. Otherwise, life will go on exactly as before, no matter how painful, unrealistic, unjust, ludicrous, or downright dumb that life may be.

The team must consist of three sorts of specialists, he says. Otherwise, the revolution, whether in politics or the arts or the sciences or whatever, is sure to fail.

The rarest of these specialists, he says, is an authentic genius—a person capable of having seemingly good ideas not in general circulation. "A genius working alone," he says, "is invariably ignored as a lunatic."

The second sort of specialist is a lot easier to find: a highly intelligent citizen in good standing in his or her community, who understands and admires the fresh ideas of the genius, and who testifies that the genius is far from mad. "A person like that working alone," says Slazinger, "can only yearn out loud for changes, but fail to say what their shapes should be."

The third sort of specialist is a person who can explain anything, no matter how complicated, to the satisfaction of most people, no matter how stupid or pigheaded they may be. "He will say almost anything in order to be interesting and exciting," says Slazinger. "Working alone, depending solely on his own shallow ideas, he would be regarded as being as full of shit as a Christmas turkey."

* * *

Slazinger, high as a kite, says that every successful revolution, including Abstract Expressionism, the one I took part in, had that cast of characters at the top— Pollock being the genius in our case, Lenin being the one in Russia's, Christ being the one in Christianity's.

He says that if you can't get a cast like that together, you can forget changing *anything* in a great big way.

* * *

Just think! This one house by the seaside, so empty and dead only a few months ago, is now giving birth to a book about how to revolt successfully, a book about how poor girls feel about rich boys, and the memoirs of a painter whose pictures all came unstuck from canvas.

And we are expecting a baby, too!

* * *

I look out my window and see a simple man astride a tractor which drags a madly chattering gang of mowers across my lawns. I know little more about him than his name is Franklin Cooley, and that he drives an old, babyshit-brown Cadillac Coupe de Ville, and has six kids. I don't even know if Mr. Cooley can read and write. At least forty million Americans can't read and write, according to this morning's *New York Times.* That is six times as many illiterates as there are people of Armenian descent anywhere! So many of them and so few of us!

Does Franklin Cooley, that poor, dumb bastard with six kids, his ears filled with the clashing gibberish of the mowers, have the least suspicion that earthshaking work is going on in here?

* * *

Yes, and guess what *else The New York Times* said this morning? Geneticists have *incontrovertible* evidence that men and women were once separate races, men evolving in Asia and women evolving in Africa. It was simply a coincidence that they were interfertile when they met.

The clitoris, so goes the speculation in the paper, is the last vestige of the inseminating organ of a conquered, enslaved, trivialized and finally emasculated race of weaker, but not necessarily dumber, anthropoids!

Cancel my subscription!

25

Back to the Great Depression! To make a long story short: Germany invaded Austria and then Czechoslovakia and then Poland and then France, and I was a pipsqueak casualty in faraway New York City. Coulomb Frères et Cie was out of business, so I lost my job at the agency—not that long after my father's Moslem obsequies. So I joined what was still a peacetime United States Army, and scored high on their classification test. The Great Depression was as discouraging as ever, and the Army was still a very little family in this country, so I was lucky to be accepted. The recruiting sergeant on Times Square, I remember, had indicated that I might be a more attractive relative in prospect if I were to have my name legally changed to something more American.

I even remember his helpful suggestion: that I become "Robert King." Just think: somebody might now be trespassing on my private beach and gazing in awe at this mansion, and wondering who could be rich enough to live this well, and the answer could so easily have been this: "Robert King."

*   *   *

But the Army adopted me as Rabo Karabekian—as I was soon to discover, for this reason: Major General Daniel Whitehall, then the commander of the combat troops of the Corps of Engineers, wanted an oil painting of himself in full uniform, and believed that somebody with a foreign-sounding name could do the best job. As an Army regular, of course, I would have to paint him for free. And this was a man ravenous for immortality. He was going to be retired in six months, by reason of failing kidneys, having barely missed service in two world wars.

God only knows what became of the portrait I did of him—after hours during basic training. I used the most expensive materials, which he was more than glad to buy for me. There is one painting of mine which might actually outlive the "Mona Lisa"! If I had realized that at the time I might have given him a puzzling half-smile, whose meaning only I knew for certain: he had become a general, but had missed the two big wars of his lifetime.

*   *   *

Another painting of mine which just might outlive the "Mona Lisa," for better or for worse, is the gigantic son of a bitch out in the potato barn.

*   *   *

So much I only *now* realize! When I did the portrait of General Whitehall in a mansion nearly as grand as this one, which was the property of the Army, I was stereotypically Armenian! Welcome home to my true nature! I was a scrawny recruit and he was a Pasha weighing more than two hundred pounds, who could squash me like an insect anytime he pleased.

But what sly and self-serving advice, but actually very good advice, too, I was able to give him along with flattery on this order: "You have a very strong chin. Did you know that?"

In what must surely have been the manner of powerless Armenian advisors in Turkish courts, I congratulated him on having ideas he might never have had before. An example: "You must be thinking very hard how important aerial photography is going to be, if war should come." War, of course, had come to practically everybody but the United States by then.

"Yes," he said.

"Would you turn your head the least little bit to the left?" I said. "Wonderful! That way there aren't such deep shadows in your eye sockets. I certainly don't want to lose those eyes. And could you imagine now that you are looking from a hilltop at sunset—over a valley where a battle is going to take place the next day?"

So he did that as best he could, and he couldn't talk without ruining everything. But, like a dentist, I was prefectly free to go on jabbering. "Good! Wonderful! Perfect! Don't move anything!" I said. And then I added almost absentmindedly as I laid the paint on: "Every branch of the service is claiming camouflage from the air as their specialty, even though it's obviously the business of the Engineers."

And I said a little later: "Artists are so naturally good at camouflage, I guess I'm just the first of many to be recruited by the Corps of Engineers."

* * *

Did such a sly and smarmy and Levantine seduction work? You be the judge:

The painting was unveiled at the General's retirement ceremonies. I had completed my basic training and been promoted to private first class. I was simply another soldier with an obsolescent Springfield rifle, standing in ranks before the bunting-draped scaffold which supported the painting on an easel, and from which the General spoke.

He lectured on aerial photography, and the clear mission of the Engineers to teach the other branches of the service about camouflage. He said that among the last orders he would ever give was one which called for all enlisted men with what he called "artistic experiences" to be assigned to a new camouflage unit under the command of, now get this: "Master Sergeant Rabo Karabekian. I hope I pronounced his name right."

He had, he *had*!

* * *

I was a master sergeant at Fort Belvoir when I read of the deaths of Dan Gregory and Fred Jones in Egypt.

There was no mention of Marilee. They had died as civilians, although in uniforms, and they both got respectful obituaries, since the United States was still a neutral nation in the war. The Italians weren't our enemies yet, and the British who killed Gregory and Fred weren't yet our allies. Gregory, I remember, was bid farewell in the papers as possibly the best-known American artist in history. Fred was sent on to Judgment Day as a World War One ace, which he wasn't, and an aviation pioneer.

I, of course, wondered what had become of Marilee. She was still young and I presumed beautiful, and had a good chance of finding some man a lot richer than I was to look after her. I was certainly in no position to make her my own. Military pay was still very low even for a master sergeant. There were no Holy Grails for sale at the Post Exchange.

*　*　*

When my country finally went to war like everybody else, I was commissioned a lieutenant and served, if not fought, in North Africa and Sicily and England and France. I was forced to fight at last on the border of Germany, and was wounded and captured without having fired a shot. There was this white flash.

The war in Europe ended on May 8, 1945. My prison camp had not yet been captured by the Russians. I, with hundreds of other captured officers from Great Britain, from France, from Belgium, from Yugoslavia, from Russia, from Italy, which country had switched sides, from Canada and New Zealand and South Africa and Australia, from everywhere, was marched at route step out of our prison and into the still-to-be-conquered countryside. Our guards vanished one night, and we awoke the next morning on the rim of a great green valley on what is now the border between East Germany and Czechoslovakia. There may have been as many as ten thousand people below us—concentration camp survivors, slave laborers, lunatics released from asylums and ordinary criminals released from jails and prisons, captured officers and enlisted men from every Army which had fought the Germans.

What a *sight*! And, if that weren't enough for a person to see and then marvel about for a lifetime, listen to this: the very last remains of Hitler's armies, their uniforms in tatters but their killing machines still in working order, were also there.

Unforgettable!

26

At the end of my war, my country, where the only person I knew was a Chinese laundryman, paid in full for cosmetic surgery performed on the place where my eye used to be. Was I bitter? No, I was simply blank, which I came to realize was what Fred Jones used to be. Neither one of us had anything to come home to.

Who paid for my eye operation at Fort Benjamin Harrison outside Indianapolis? He was a tall, skinny fellow, tough but fair-minded, plain spoken but shrewd. No, I am not speaking of Santa Claus, whose image in shopping malls at Christmas time nowadays is largely based on a painting Dan Gregory made for *Liberty* magazine in 1923. No. I am speaking of my Uncle Sam.

* * *

As I've said, I married my nurse at the hospital. As I've said, we had two sons who no longer speak to me. They aren't even Karabekians anymore. They had their last names legally changed to that of their stepfather, whose name was Roy Steel.

Terry Kitchen asked me one time why, since I had so few gifts as a husband and father, I had gotten married. And I heard myself say: "That's the way the postwar movie goes."

That conversation must have taken place about five years after the war.

The two of us must have been lying on cots I had bought for the studio space we had rented above Union Square. That loft had become not only Kitchen's workplace but his home. I myself had taken to spending two or three nights a week there, as I found myself less and less beloved in the basement apartment three blocks away, where my wife and children lived.

* * *

What did my wife have to complain about? I had quit my job as a salesman of life insurance for Connecticut General. I was intoxicated most of the time not only by alcohol but by the creation of huge fields of a single color of Sateen Dura-Luxe. I had rented a potato barn and made a down payment on a house out here, which was then a wilderness.

And in the midst of that domestic nightmare there arrived a registered letter from Italy, a country I had never seen. It asked me to come to Florence, all expenses paid for one, to testify in a lawsuit there about two paintings, a Giotto and a Masaccio, which had been taken by American soldiers from a German general in Paris. They had been turned over to my platoon of art experts to be catalogued and shipped to a warehouse in Le Havre, where they were to be crated and stored. The general had evidently stolen them from a private house while retreating north through Florence.

The crating in Le Havre was done by Italian prisoners of war, who had done that sort of work in civilian life. One of them evidently found a way to ship both paintings to his wife in Rome, where he kept them hidden, except to show to close friends after the war. The rightful owners were suing to recover them.

So I went over there alone, and I got my name in the papers for accounting for the trip the paintings made from Paris to Le Havre.

*   *   *

But I had a secret, which I have never told anybody before: "Once an illustrator, always an illustrator!" I couldn't help seeing stories in my own compositions of strips of colored tape applied to vast, featureless fields of Sateen Dura-Luxe. This idea came into my head uninvited, like a nitwit tune for a singing commercial, and would not get out again; each strip of tape was the soul at the core of some sort of person or lower animal.

So whenever I stuck on a piece of tape, the voice of the illustrator in me who would not die would say, for example, "The orange tape is the soul of an Arctic explorer, separated from his companions, and the white one is the soul of a charging polar bear."

This secret fantasy, moreover, infected and continues to infect my way of seeing scenes in real life. If I watch two people talking on a street corner, I see not only their flesh and clothes, but narrow, vertical bands of color inside them—not so much like tape, actually, but more like low-intensity neon tubes.

* * *

When I got back to my hotel at about noon on my last day in Florence, there was a note for me in my pigeonhole. As far as I knew, I had no friends in all of Italy. The note on expensive paper with a noble crest at the top said this:

> *There can't be all that many Rabo Karabekians in the world. If you're the wrong one, come on over anyway. I'm mad for Armenians. Isn't everybody? You can rub your feet on my carpets and make sparks. Sound like fun? Down with modern art! Wear something green.*

And it was signed, *Marilee, Countess Portomaggiore (the coal miner's daughter).*
Wow!

27

I telephoned her at once from the hotel. She asked if I could come to tea in an hour! I said I sure *could*! My heart was beating like mad!

She was only four blocks away—in a palazzo designed for Innocenzo "the Invisible" de Medici by Leon Battista Alberti in the middle of the fifteenth century. It was a cruciform structure whose four wings abutted on a domed rotunda twelve meters in diameter and in whose walls were half embedded eighteen Corinthian columns four and a half meters high. Above the capitals of the columns was a clerestory, a wall pierced with thirty-six windows. Above this was the dome—on whose underside was an epiphany, God Almighty and Jesus and the Virgin Mary and angels looking down through clouds, painted by Paolo Uccello. The terrazzo floor, its designer unknown, but almost surely a Venetian, was decorated with the backs of peasants planting and harvesting and cooking and baking and making wine and so on.

* * *

The incomparable Rabo Karabekian is not here demonstrating his connoisseurship nor his Armenian gift for total recall—nor his fluency with the metric system, for that matter. All the information above comes from a brand new book published by Alfred A. Knopf, Incorporated, called *Private Art Treasures of Tuscany,* with text and photographs by a South Korean political exile named Kim Bum Suk. According to the preface, it was originally Kim Bum Suk's doctoral thesis for a degree in the history of architecture from Massachusetts Institute of Technology. He managed to examine and photograph the interiors of many opulent private homes in and around Florence which few scholars had ever seen, and whose art treasures had never before been photographed by an outsider or noted in any public catalogue.

Among these hitherto impenetrable private spaces was, hey presto, the palazzo of Innocenzo "the Invisible" de Medici, which I myself penetrated thirty-seven years ago.

* * *

The palazzo and its contents, uninterruptedly private property for five and a half centuries now, remains private property, following the death of my friend, Marilee, Contessa Portomaggiore, who was the person who, according to the book, gave Kim Bum Suk and his camera and his metric measuring instruments the run of the place. Ownership, upon Marilee's death two years ago, passed on to her late husband's nearest male blood relative, a second cousin, an automobile dealer in Milan, who sold it at once to an Egyptian man of mystery, believed to be an arms dealer. His name? Hold on to your hats: his name is Leo *Mamigonian!*

Small World!

He is the son of Vartan Mamigonian, the man who diverted my parents from Paris to San Ignacio, and who cost me an eye, among other things. How could I ever forgive Vartan Mamigonian?

* * *

Leo Mamigonian bought all the contents of the palazzo, too, and so must own Marilee's collection of Abstract Expressionist paintings, which was the best in Europe, and second in the world only to mine.

What is it about Armenians that they always *do* so well? There should be an investigation.

* * *

How did I come to possess Kim Bum Suk's invaluable doctoral thesis at precisely the moment I must write about my reunion with Marilee in 1950? We have here another coincidence, which superstitious persons would no doubt take seriously.

Two days ago, the widow Berman, made vivacious and supranaturally alert by God only knows what postwar pharmaceutical miracles, entered the bookstore in

East Hampton, and heard, by her own account, one book out of hundreds calling out to her. It said that I would like it. So she bought it for me.

She had no way of knowing that I was on the brink of writing about Florence. Nobody did. She gave me the book without herself examining the contents, and so did not know that my old girlfriend's palazzo was therein described.

One would soon go mad if one took such coincidences too seriously. One might be led to suspect that there were all sorts of things going on in the Universe which he or she did not thoroughly understand.

*　*　*

Dr. Kim or Dr. Bum or Dr. Suk, whichever is the family name, if any, has cleared up two questions I had about the rotunda when I myself was privileged to see it. The first puzzle was how the dome was filled with natural light in the daytime. It turns out that there were mirrors on the sills of the clerestory windows— and there were still more mirrors on the roofs outside to capture sunbeams and deflect them upward into the dome.

The second puzzle was this: why were the vast rectangles between the encircling columns at ground level blank? How could any art patron have left them bare? When I saw them, they were painted the palest rose-orange, not unlike the Sateen Dura-Luxe shade yclept "Maui Eventide."

Dr. Kim or Dr. Bum or Dr. Suk explains that lightly clad pagan gods and goddesses used to cavort in these spaces, and that they were lost forever. They had not been merely concealed under coats of paint. They had

been *scraped* off the walls during the exile of the
Medicis from Florence from 1494, two years after the
discovery of this hemisphere by white people, until
1531. The murals were destroyed by the insistence of
the Dominican monk Girolamo Savonarola, who
wished to dispel every trace of paganism, which he felt
had poisoned the city during the reign of the Medicis.

The murals were the work of Giovanni Vitelli, about
whom almost nothing else is known, except that he was
said to have been born in Pisa. One may assume that he
was the Rabo Karabekian of his time, and that Christian
fundamentalism was his Sateen Dura-Luxe.

* * *

Kim Bum Suk, incidentally, was thrown out of his
native South Korea for forming a union of university
students which demanded improvements in the curric-
ula.

Girolamo Savonarola, incidentally, was hanged and
burned in the piazza in front of what had been the
Palazzo of Innocenzo "the Invisible" de Medici in 1494.

I sure love history. I don't know why Celeste and her
friends aren't more interested.

* * *

I now think of the rotunda of that palazzo, when it
still had its pagan as well as its Christian images, as a
Renaissance effort to make an atom bomb. It cost a
great deal of money and employed many of the best
minds of the time, and it compressed into a small space
and in bizarre combinations the most powerful forces
of the Universe as the Universe was understood in the
fifteenth century.

The Universe has certainly come a long, long way since then.

* * *

As for Innocenzo "the Invisible" de Medici, according to Kim Bum Suk: he was a banker, which I choose to translate as "loan shark and extortionist" or "gangster," in the parlance of the present day. He was simultaneously the richest and least public member of his family. No portrait of him was ever made, save for a bust done of him when a child by the sculptor Lorenzo Ghiberti. He himself smashed that bust when he was fifteen years old, and threw the pieces into the Arno. He attended no parties and gave none when an adult, and never traveled in the city save in a conveyance which hid him from view.

After his palazzo was completed, his most trusted henchmen and even the highest dignitaries, including two of his own cousins who were Popes, never saw him save in the rotunda. They were obliged to stand at the edge of it, while he alone occupied the middle—wearing a shapeless monk's robe and a death's-head mask.

* * *

He drowned while in exile in Venice. This was long before the invention of water wings.

* * *

When Marilee told me on the telephone to come over to her palazzo right away, the tone of her voice, coupled with her confession that there were no men in her life just then, seemed guarantees to me that in no more than two hours, probably, I would be getting more of the greatest loving I had ever had—and not as a callow youth this time, but as a war hero, roué, and seasoned cosmopolite!

I in turn warned her that I had lost an eye in battle, and so would be wearing an eye patch, and that I was married, yes, but that the marriage was on the rocks.

I am afraid that I said, too, in making light of my years as a warrior, that I had spent most of my time ". . . combing pussy out of my hair." This meant that women had made themselves available to me in great numbers. This odd locution was a variant of a metaphor which made a lot more sense: a person who had been shelled a great deal might say that he had been combing tree bursts out of his hair.

So I arrived at the appointed hour in a twanging state of vanity and concupiscence. I was led by a female servant down a long, straight corridor to the edge of the rotunda. All the Contessa Portomaggiore's servants were females—even the porters and gardeners. The one who let me in, I remember, struck me as mannish and unfriendly—and then downright military when she told me to stop just inside the rotunda.

* * *

At the center, clad from neck to floor in the deepest black mourning for her husband, Count Bruno—there stood Marilee.

She wasn't wearing a death's-head mask, but her face was so pale and in the dim light so close to the color of her flaxen hair that her head might have been carved from a single piece of old ivory.

I was aghast.

Her voice was imperious and scornful. "So, my faithless little Armenian protégé," she said, "we meet again."

28

"Thought you were going to get laid again, I'll bet," she said. Her words echoed whisperingly in the dome—as though they were being discussed up there by the Divinities.

"Surprise, surprise," she said, "we're not even going to shake hands today."

I wagged my head in unhappy wonderment. "Why are you so mad at me?" I asked.

"During the Great Depression," she said, "I thought you were the one real friend I had in the world. And then we made love, and I never heard from you again."

"I can't believe this," I said. "You told me to go away —for the good of *both* of us. Have you forgotten that?"

"You must have been awfully glad to hear me say that," she said. "You sure went away."

"What did you *expect* me to do?" I said.

"To give some sign, any sign, that you cared how I was," she said. "You've had fourteen years to do it, but you never did it—not one telephone call, not one postcard. Now here you are back like a bad penny: expecting what? Expecting to get laid again."

* * *

"You mean we could have gone on being lovers?" I asked incredulously.

"Lovers? Lovers? Lovers?" she mocked me raucously. The echoes of her scorn for lovers sounded like warring blackbirds overhead.

"There's never been any shortage of lovers for Marilee Kemp," she said. "My father loved me so much he beat me every day. The football team at the high school loved me so much they raped me all night after the Junior Prom. The stage manager at the Ziegfield Follies loved me so much he told me that I had to be part of his stable of whores or he'd fire me and have somebody throw acid in my face. Dan Gregory loved me so much he threw me down the stairs because I'd sent you some expensive art materials."

"He did *what?*" I said.

So she told me the true story of how I had become the apprentice of Dan Gregory.

I was flabbergasted. "But—but he must have liked my pictures, didn't he?" I stammered.

"No," she said.

* * *

"That's one beating I took on account of you," she said. "I took another one after we made love and I never heard from you again. Now let's talk about all the wonderful things you did for me."

"I never felt so ashamed in my life," I said.

"All right—I'll tell you what you did for me: you went for happy, silly, beautiful walks with me."

"Yes—" I said, "I remember those."

"You used to rub your feet on the carpets and then give me shocks on my neck when I least expected it," she said.

"Yes," I said.

"And we were so naughty sometimes," she said.

"When we made love," I said.

She blew up again. "No! No! No! You jerk! You jerk! You incomparable jerk!" she exclaimed. "The Museum of Modern Art!"

* * *

"So you lost an eye in the war," she said.

"So did Fred Jones," I said.

"So did Lucrezia and Maria," she said.

"Who are they?" I said.

"My cook," she said, "and the woman who let you in."

* * *

"Did you win a lot of medals in the war?" she said.

Actually, I hadn't done too badly. I had a *Bronze Star* with a *Cluster*, and a *Purple Heart* for my wound, and a *Presidential Unit Citation*, a *Soldier's Medal*, a *Good Conduct Badge*, and a *European-African-Middle Eastern Campaign Ribbon* with seven *Battle Stars*.

I was proudest of my *Soldier's Medal*, which is usually

awarded to a soldier who has saved the life of another soldier in situations not necessarily related to combat. In 1941, I was giving a course in camouflage techniques to officer candidates at Fort Benning, Georgia. I saw a barracks on fire, and I gave the alarm, and then went in twice, without regard for my own safety, and carried out two unconscious enlisted men.

They were the only two people in there, and nobody was supposed to be in there. They had been drinking, and had accidentally started the fire themselves, for which they were given two years at hard labor—plus loss of all pay and dishonorable discharges.

About my medals: all I said to Marilee was that I guessed I had received my share.

How Terry Kitchen used to envy me for my Soldier's Medal, incidentally. He had a Silver Star, and he said a Soldier's Medal was worth ten of those.

* * *

"Whenever I see a man wearing a medal," said Marilee, "I want to cry and hug him, and say, 'Oh, you poor baby—all the terrible things you've *been* through, just so the woman and the children could be safe at home.' "

She said she used to want to go up to Mussolini, who had so many medals that they covered both sides of his tunic right down to his belt, and say to him, "After all you've been through, how can there be anything *left* of you?"

And then she brought up the unfortunate expression I had used when talking to her on the telephone: "Did you say that in the war you were 'combing pussy out of your hair'?"

I said I was sorry I'd said it, and I was.

"I never heard that expression before," she said. "I had to guess what it meant."

"Just forget I said it," I said.

"You want to know what my guess was? I guessed that wherever you went there were women who would do anything for food or protection for themselves and the children and the old people, since the young men were dead or gone away," she said. "How close was I?"

"Oh my, oh my, oh my," I said.

"What's the matter, Rabo?" she said.

"You hit the nail on the head," I said.

* * *

"Wasn't very hard to guess," she said. "The whole point of war is to put women everywhere in that condition. It's always men against women, with the men only pretending to fight among themselves."

"They can pretend pretty hard sometimes," I said.

"They know that the ones who pretend the hardest," she said, "get their pictures in the paper and medals afterwards."

* * *

"Do you have an artificial leg?" she said.

"No," I said.

"Lucrezia, the woman who let you in, lost a leg along with her eye. I thought maybe you'd lost one, too."

"No such luck," I said.

"Well—" she said, "early one morning she crossed a meadow, carrying two precious eggs to a neighbor who had given birth to a baby the night before. She stepped on a mine. We don't know what army was responsible.

We do know the sex. Only a male would design and bury a device that ingenious. Before you leave, maybe you can persuade Lucrezia to show you all the medals she won."

And then she added: "Women are so useless and unimaginative, aren't they? All they ever think of planting in the dirt is the seed of something beautiful or edible. The only missile they can ever think of throwing at anybody is a ball or a bridal bouquet."

I said with utmost fatigue, "O.K., Marilee—you've certainly made your point. I have never felt worse in my life. I only wish the Arno were deep enough to drown myself in. Can I please return to my hotel?"

"No," she said. "I think I've reduced you to the level of self-esteem which men try to force on women. If I have, I would very much like to have you stay for the tea I promised you. Who knows? We might even become friends again."

29

Marilee led me to a small and cozy library which used to house, she said, her late husband's great collection of male homosexual pornography. I asked her what had become of the books, and she said she had sold them for a great deal of money, which she had divided among her servants—all women who had been badly hurt one way or another by war.

We settled into overstuffed chairs, facing each other across a coffee table. She beamed at me fondly and then said this: "Well, well, well, my young protégé—how goes it? Long time no see. Marriage on the rocks, you say?"

"I'm sorry I said that," I said. "I'm sorry I said any-thing. I feel like something the cat drug in."

We were served tea and little cakes at that point by a woman who had two steel clamps where her hands should have been. Marilee said something to her in Italian, and she laughed.

"What did you say to her?" I asked.

"I said your marriage was on the rocks," she said.

The woman with the clamps said something to her in Italian, and I requested a translation.

"She said you should marry a man next time," said Marilee.

"Her husband plunged her hands into boiling water," she said, "in order to make her tell him who her lovers had been while he was away at war. They were Ger-mans and then Americans, by the way, and gangrene set in."

*   *   *

Over the fireplace of Marilee's cozy library was the Dan Gregory–style painting I mentioned earlier, a gift to her from the people of Florence: showing her late husband, Count Bruno, refusing a blindfold while fac-ing a firing squad. She said that it hadn't happened exactly that way, but that nothing ever did. So I asked her how it happened that she became the Contessa Portomaggiore, with the beautiful palazzo and rich farms to the north and so on.

When she and Gregory and Fred Jones arrived in Italy, she said, before the United States got into the war, and against Italy and Germany and Japan, they were received as great celebrities. They represented a pro-paganda victory for Mussolini: " 'America's greatest living artist and one of its greatest aviators and the incomparably beautiful and gifted American actress, Marilee Kemp,' he called us," said Marilee. "He said the three of us had come to take part in the spiritual and physical and economic miracle in Italy, which would become the model for the world for thousands of years to come."

The propaganda value of the three of them was so great that she was accorded in the press and at social events the respect a real and famous actress deserved. "So suddenly I wasn't a dim-witted floozy anymore," she said. "I was a jewel in the crown of the new Roman emperor. Dan and Fred, I must say, found this confusing. They had no choice in public but to treat me more respectfully, and I had fun with that. This country is absolutely crazy about blondes, of course, so that, whenever we had to make an entrance, I came first—and they came along behind me, as part of my entourage.

"And it was somehow very easy for me to learn Italian," she said. "I was soon better at it than Dan, who'd taken lessons in it back in New York. Fred, of course, never learned Italian at all."

* * *

Fred and Dan became heroes in Italy after they died fighting more or less for the Italian cause. Marilee's celebrity survived them—as a very beautiful and charming reminder of their supreme sacrifice, and of the admiration many Americans had, supposedly, for Mussolini.

She was still certainly beautiful, by the way, at the time of our reunion, even without makeup and in widow's weeds. She should have been an old lady after all she had been through, but she was only forty-three. She had a third of a century still to go!

And, as I say, she would become Europe's largest Sony distributor, among other things. There was life in the old girl yet!

The Contessa was surely way ahead of her time, too, in believing that men were not only useless and idiotic, but downright dangerous. That idea wouldn't catch on big in her native country until the last three years of the Vietnam War.

*   *   *

After Dan Gregory's death, her regular escort in Rome was Mussolini's Oxford-educated and unmarried Minister of Culture, the handsome Bruno, Count Portomaggiore. He explained to Marilee at once that they could have no physical relationship, since he was interested sexually only in men and boys. Such a preference, if acted upon, was a capital offense at the time, but Count Bruno felt perfectly safe, no matter how outrageously he might behave. He was confident that Mussolini would protect him, since he was the only member of the old aristocracy who had accepted a high position in his government, and who virtually wallowed in admiration at the upstart dictator's booted feet.

"He was a perfect ass," said Marilee. She said that people laughed at his cowardice and vanity and effeminacy.

"He was also," she added, "the perfect head of British Intelligence in Italy."

*   *   *

After Dan and Fred were killed, and before the United States got into the war, Marilee was the toast of Rome. She had a wonderful time shopping and dancing, dancing, dancing, with the count, who enjoyed hearing her talk, and was always the perfect gentleman. Her wish was his command, and he never threatened her physically, and never demanded that she do this or that until one night, when he told her that Mussolini himself had ordered him to marry her!

"He had many enemies," said Marilee, "and they had been telling Mussolini that he was a homosexual and a British spy. Mussolini certainly knew he loved men and boys, but didn't even suspect that a man that silly could have the nerve or wit to be a spy."

When Mussolini ordered his Minister of Culture to prove that he wasn't a homosexual by wedding Marilee, he also handed him a document for Marilee to sign. It was designed to placate old aristocrats to whom the idea of an American floozy's inheriting ancient estates would have been intolerable. It set forth that, in the case of the count's death, Marilee would have his property for life, but without the right to sell it or leave it to anyone else. Upon her death, it was to go to the count's nearest male relative, who, as I have said, turned out to be an automobile dealer in Milan.

The next day, the Japanese in a surprise attack sank a major fraction of the United States warships at Pearl Harbor, leaving this still pacifistic, antimilitaristic country no choice but to declare war on not only Japan, but on Japan's allies, Germany and Italy, as well.

*　*　*

But even before Pearl Harbor, Marilee told the only man ever to propose marriage to her, and a rich nobleman at that, that no, she would not marry him. She thanked him for happiness such as she had never known before. She said that his proposal and the accompanying document had awakened her from what could only be a dream, and that it was time for her to return to the United States, where she could try to deal with who and what she really was, even though she didn't have a home there.

But then, all excited the next morning about going home, Marilee found the spiritual climate of Rome, although the real Sun was shining brightly and the real clouds were somewhere else, to be as dark and chilling as, and this is how she described it to me in Florence, "rain and sleet at midnight."

* * *

Marilee listened to the news about Pearl Harbor on the radio that morning. One item was about the approximately seven thousand American citizens living in Italy. The American Embassy, which was still operating, still technically at peace with Italy, announced that it was making plans to provide transportation back to the United States for as many as possible, as soon as possible. The Italian government responded that it would do all within its power to facilitate their departure, but that there was surely no reason for a mass exodus, since Italy and the United States had close bonds of both blood and history which should not be broken in order to satisfy the demands of Jews and Communists and the decaying British Empire.

Marilee's personal maid came in with the quotidian

announcement that some sort of workman wanted to talk to her about the possibility of old, leaking gas pipes in her bedroom, and he wore coveralls and had a toolbox. He tapped the walls and sniffed, and murmured to himself in Italian. And then, when the two of them were surely alone, he began, still facing the wall, to speak softly in middle-western American English.

He said that he was from the War Department of the United States, which is what the Department of Defense used to be called. We had no separate spy organization back then. He said that he had no idea how she felt down deep about democracy or fascism, but that it was his duty to ask her, for the good of their country, to remain in Italy and to continue to curry the favor of Mussolini's government.

By her own account, Marilee then thought about democracy and fascism for the first time in her life. She decided that democracy sounded better.

"Why should I stay here and do that?" she asked.

"Sooner or later, you might hear something we would be very interested in knowing," he said. "Sooner or later, or even possibly never, your country might have some use to make of you."

She said to him that the whole world suddenly seemed to be going crazy.

He commented that there was nothing sudden about it, that it had belonged in a prison or a lunatic asylum for quite some time.

As an example of what she saw as sudden craziness, she told him about Mussolini's ordering his minister of culture to marry her.

He replied, according to Marilee: "If you have one

atom of love for America in your heart, you will marry him."

Thus did a coal miner's daughter become the Contessa Portomaggiore.

30

Marilee did not learn until the war was nearly over that her husband was a British agent. She, too, thought him a weakling and a fool, but forgave him that since they lived so well and he was so nice to her. "He had the most amusing and kind and flattering things to say to me. He really enjoyed my company. We both loved to dance and dance."

So there was another woman in my life with a mania for dancing, who would do it with anybody as long as they did it well.

"You never danced with Dan Gregory," I said.

"He wouldn't," she said, "and you wouldn't either."

"I couldn't," I said. "I never had."

"Anybody who wants to can," she said.

*   *   *

She said that the news that her husband was a British spy made almost no impression on her. "He had all these uniforms for different occasions, and I never cared what any of them were supposed to mean. They were covered with emblems which I never bothered to decode. I never asked him: 'Bruno, what did you get this medal for? What does the eagle on your sleeve mean? What are those two crosses on your collar points?' So when he told me that he was a British spy, that was just more of the junk jewelry of warfare. It had almost nothing to do with me or him."

She said that after he was shot she expected to feel a terrible emptiness, but did not. And then she understood that her real companion and mate for life was the Italian people. "They spoke to me so lovingly wherever I went, Rabo, and I loved them in return, and did not give a damn about what junk jewelry they wore!"

"I'm *home*, Rabo," she said. "I never would have got here if it hadn't been for the craziness of Dan Gregory. Thanks to loose screws in the head of an Armenian from Moscow, I'm home, I'm home."

*   *   *

"Now tell me what *you've* been doing with all these years," she said.

"For some reason I find myself dismayingly uninteresting," I said.

"Oh, come, come, come," she said. "You lost an eye, you married, you reproduced twice, and you say you've taken up painting again. How could a life be more eventful?"

I thought to myself that there had been events, but very few, certainly, since our Saint Patrick's Day love-making so long ago, which had made me proud and happy. I had old soldier's anecdotes I had told my drinking buddies in the Cedar Tavern, so I told her those. She had had a life. I had accumulated anecdotes. She was home. Home was somewhere I never thought I'd be.

*　*　*

Old Soldier's Anecdote Number One: "While Paris was being liberated," I said, "I went to find Pablo Picasso, Dan Gregory's idea of Satan—to make sure he was O.K.," I said.

"He opened his door a crack, with a chain across it inside, and said he was busy and did not wish to be disturbed. You could still hear guns going off only a couple of blocks away. Then he shut and locked the door again."

Marilee laughed and said, "Maybe he knew all the terrible things our lord and master used to say about him." She said that if she had known I was still alive, she would have saved a picture in an Italian magazine which only she and I could fully appreciate. It showed a collage Picasso had made by cutting up a poster advertising American cigarettes. He had reassembled pieces of the poster, which originally showed three cowboys smoking around a campfire at night, to form a cat.

Of all the art experts on Earth, only Marilee and I,

most likely, could identify the painter of the mutilated poster as Dan Gregory.

How is that for trivia?

*　*　*

"So that is probably the only point at which Picasso paid the least bit of attention to one of the most popular American artists in history," I speculated.

"Probably," she said.

*　*　*

Old Soldier's Anecdote Number Two: "I was captured when the war had only a few more months to go," I said. "I was patched up in a hospital and then sent to a camp south of Dresden, where they were practically out of food. Everything in what was left of Germany had been eaten up. So we were all getting skinnier and skinnier except for the man we'd elected to divide what food there was into equal shares.

"There was never a time when he had the food to himself. We saw it delivered, and then he divided it up with all of us watching. Still, he somehow remained sleek and contented-looking while the rest of us became skeletons.

"He was feasting absentmindedly on crumbs and dribblings that fell on the tabletop and clung to his knife and ladle."

This same innocent phenomenon, by the way, explains the great prosperity of many of my neighbors up and down the beach here. They are in charge of such wealth as remains in this generally bankrupt country, since they are so *trustworthy.* A little bit of it is bound to try to find its way to their mouths from their busy fingers and implements.

* * *

Old Soldier's Anecdote Number Three: "One evening in May," I said, "we were marched out of our camp and into the countryside. We were halted at about three in the morning, and told to sleep under the stars as best we could.

"When we awoke at sunrise, the guards were gone, and we found that we were on the rim of a valley near the ruins of an ancient stone watchtower. Below us, in that innocent farmland, were thousands upon thousands of people like us, who had been brought there by their guards, had been *dumped*. These weren't only prisoners of war. They were people who had been marched out of concentration camps and factories where they had been slaves, and out of regular prisons for criminals, and out of lunatic asylums. The idea was to turn us loose as far as possible from the cities, where we might raise hell.

"And there were civilians there, too, who had run and run from the Russian front or the American and British front. The fronts had actually met to the north and south of us.

"And there were hundreds in German uniforms, with their weapons still in working order, but docile now, waiting for whomever they were expected to surrender to."

"The Peaceable Kingdom," said Marilee.

* * *

I changed the subject from war to peace. I told Marilee that I had returned to the arts after a long hiatus, and had, to my own astonishment, become a creator of serious paintings which would make Dan Gregory turn over in his hero's grave in Egypt, paintings such as the world had never seen before.

She protested in mock horror. "Oh, please—not the arts again," she said. "They're a swamp I'll never get out of as long as I live."

But she listened thoughtfully when I told her about our little gang in New York City, whose paintings were nothing alike except for one thing: they were about nothing but themselves.

When I was all talked out, she sighed, and she shook her head. "It was the last conceivable thing a painter could do to a canvas, so you *did* it," she said. "Leave it to Americans to write, 'The End.' "

"I hope that's not what we're doing," I said.

"I hope very much that it *is* what you're doing," she said. "After all that men have done to the women and children and every other defenseless thing on this planet, it is time that not just every painting, but every piece of music, every statue, every play, every poem and book a man creates, should say only this: 'We are much too horrible for this nice place. We give up. We quit. The end!' "

*   *   *

She said that our unexpected reunion was a stroke of luck for her, since she thought I might have brought the solution to an interior decorating problem which had been nagging at her for years, namely: what sort of pictures, if any, should she put on the inane blanks between the columns of her rotunda? "I want to leave some sort of mark on this place while I have it," she said, "and the rotunda seems the place to do it.

"I considered hiring women and children to paint murals of the death camps and the bombing of Hiroshima and the planting of land mines, and maybe the burning of witches and the feeding of Christians to wild animals in olden times," she said. "But I think that sort of thing, on some level, just eggs men on to be even more destructive and cruel, makes them think: 'Ha! We are as powerful as gods! There has never been anything to stop us from doing even the most frightful things, if even the most frightful things are what we *choose* to do.'

"So your idea is a much better one, Rabo. Let men come into my rotunda, and wherever they look at eye level let them receive no encouragement. Let the walls cry out: 'The end! The end!' "

*   *   *

Thus began the second great collection of American Abstract Expressionist art—the first being my own, the storage bills for which were making paupers of me and my wife and children. Nobody else wanted those pictures at any price!

Marilee ordered ten of them sight unseen—to be selected by me and at one thousand dollars each!

"You're joking!" I said.

"The Countess Portomaggiore never jokes," she said. "And I'm as noble and rich as anybody who ever lived here, so you do what I say."

So I did.

*   *   *

She asked if our gang had come up with a name for ourselves, and we hadn't. It was critics who would finally name us. She said that we should call ourselves the "Genesis Gang," since we were going right back to the beginning, when subject matter had yet to be created.

I found that a good idea, and would try to sell it to the others when I got home. But it never caught on somehow.

*   *   *

Marilee and I talked for hours, until it was dark outside. She said at last, "I think you had better go now."

"Sounds like what you said to me on Saint Patrick's Day fourteen years ago," I said.

"I hope you won't be so quick to forget me this time," she said.

"I never did that," I said.

"You forgot to *worry* about me," she said.

"I give you my word of honor, Contessa," I said, standing. "I can never do that again."

That was the last time we met. We exchanged several letters, though. I have dug one of hers from the archives here. It is dated three years after our reunion, June 7, 1953, and says that we have failed to paint pictures of nothing after all, that she easily identifies chaos in every canvas. This is a pleasant joke, of course. "Tell that to the rest of the Genesis Gang," she says.

I answered that letter with a cable, of which I have a copy. "NOT EVEN CHAOS IS SUPPOSED TO BE THERE," it reads. "WE'LL COME OVER AND PAINT IT OUT. ARE OUR FACES RED. SAINT PATRICK."

* * *

Bulletin from the present: Paul Slazinger has voluntarily committed himself to the psychiatric ward at the Veterans Administration hospital over at Riverhead. I certainly didn't know what to do about the bad chemicals his body was dumping into his bloodstream, and he was becoming a maniac even to himself. Mrs. Berman was glad to see him *out* of here.

Better he should be looked after by his Uncle Sam.

31

Of all the things I have to be ashamed of, the most troublesome of this old heart of mine is my failure as a husband of the good and brave Dorothy, and the consequent alienation of my own flesh and blood, Henri and Terry, from me, their Dad.

What will be found written after the name of Rabo Karabekian in the Big Book on Judgment Day?

"Soldier: Excellent.

"Husband and Father: Floparroo.

"Serious artist: Floparroo."

* * *

There was Hell to pay when I got home from Florence. The good and brave Dorothy and both boys had a brand new kind of influenza, yet another postwar miracle. A doctor had been to see them and would come again, and a woman upstairs was feeding them. It was agreed that I could only be in the way until Dorothy got back to her feet, and that I should spend the next few nights at the studio Terry Kitchen and I had rented above Union Square.

How smart we would have been to have me stay away for a hundred years instead!

"Before I go, I want to tell you I've got some really good news," I said.

"We're not going to move out to that godforsaken house in the middle of nowhere?" she said.

"That isn't it," I said. "You and the kids will get to love it out there, with the ocean and lots of fresh air."

"Somebody's offered you a steady job out there?" she said.

"No," I said.

"But you're going to look for one," she said. "You're going to take your degree in business administration that we all sacrificed so much for, and knock on doors out there till somebody in some decent business hires you, so we'll have steady money coming in."

"Honeybunch, listen to me," I said. "When I was in Florence I sold ten thousand dollars' worth of paintings."

Our basement apartment resembled a storage room for scenery in a theater, there were so many huge canvases in there—which I had accepted in lieu of repayments of debts. So she got off this joke: "Then you're going to end up in prison," she said, "because we don't even have three dollars' worth of paintings here."

I had made her so unhappy that she had developed a sense of humor, which she certainly didn't have when I married her.

*　　*　　*

"You're supposed to be thirty-four years old," she said. She herself was twenty-three!

"I *am* thirty-four," I said.

"Then *act* thirty-four," she said. "Act like a man with a wife and family who'll be forty before he knows it, and nobody will give him a job doing anything but sacking groceries or pumping gas."

"That's really laying it on the line, isn't it?" I said.

"I don't lay it on the line like that," she said. "Life lays it on the line like that. Rabo! What's happened to the man I married? We had such sensible plans for such a sensible life. And then you met these people—these bums."

"I always wanted to be an artist," I said.

"You never told me that," she said.

"I didn't think it was possible," I said. "Now I do."

"Too late—and much too risky for a family man. Wake up!" she said. "Why can't you just be happy with a nice family? Everybody else is."

"I'll tell you again: I sold ten thousand dollars' worth of paintings in Florence," I said.

"That'll fall through like everything else," she said.

"If you loved me, you'd have more faith in me as a painter," I said.

"I love you, but I hate your friends and your paintings," she said, "and I'm scared for me and my babies, the way things are going. The war is *over*, Rabo!"

"What is *that* supposed to mean?" I said.

"You don't have to do wild things, great big things, dangerous things that don't have a chance," she said. "You've already got all the medals anybody could want. You don't have to conquer France." This last was a reference to our grandiose talk about making New York City rather than Paris the Art Capital of the World.

"They were on our side anyway, weren't they?" she said. "Why do you have to go conquer them? What did they ever do to you?"

I was already outside the apartment when she asked me that, so all she had to do to end the conversation was what Picasso had done to me, which was to close the door and lock it.

I could hear her crying inside. Poor soul! Poor soul!

*   *   *

It was late afternoon. I took my suitcase over to Kitchen's and my studio. Kitchen was asleep on his cot. Before I woke him up, I had a look at what he had been doing in my absence. He had slashed all his paintings with an ivory-handled straight razor inherited from his paternal grandfather, who had been president of the New York Central Railroad. The Art World certainly wasn't any the poorer for what he had done. I had the obvious thought: "It's a miracle he didn't slash his wrists as well."

This was a great big beautiful Anglo-Saxon sleeping there, like Fred Jones a model for a Dan Gregory illustration of a story about an ideal American hero. And when he and I went places together, we really *did* look

like Jones and Gregory. Not only that, but Kitchen
treated me as respectfully as Fred had treated Gregory,
which was preposterous! Fred had been a genuine,
dumb, sweet lunk, whereas my own buddy, sleeping
there, was a graduate of Yale Law School, could have
been a professional pianist or tennis player or golfer.

He had inherited a world of talent along with that
straight razor. His father was a first-rate cellist and
chess player and horticulturalist, as well as a corpora-
tion lawyer and a pioneer in winning civil rights for the
black people.

My sleeping buddy had also outranked me in the
Army, as a lieutenant colonel in the Paratroops, and in
deeds of derring-do! But he chose to stand in awe of me
because I could do one thing he could never do, which
was to draw or paint a likeness of anything my eye
could see.

As for my own work there in the studio, the big fields
of color before which I could stand intoxicated for hour
after hour: they were meant to be *beginnings*. I expected them to become more and more complicated as
I slowly but surely closed in on what had so long eluded
me: soul, soul, soul.

* * *

I woke him up, and said I would buy him an early
supper at the Cedar Tavern. I didn't tell him about the
big deal I had pulled off in Florence, since he couldn't
be a part of it. He wouldn't get his hands on the spray
rig for two more days.

When the Contessa Portomaggiore died, incidentally, her collection would include *sixteen* Terry Kitchens.

* * *

"Early supper" meant early drinking too. There were already three painters at what had become our regular table in the back. I will call them "Painters X, Y and Z." And, lest I give aid and comfort to Philistines eager to hear that the first Abstract Expressionists were a bunch of drunks and wild men, let me say who these three *weren't.*

They were *not,* repeat, were *not:* William Baziotes, James Brooks, Willem de Kooning, Arshile Gorky, who was already dead by then anyway, Adolph Gottlieb, Philip Guston, Hans Hofmann, Barnett Newman, Jackson Pollock, Ad Reinhardt, Mark Rothko, Clyfford Still, Syd Solomon or Bradley Walker Tomlin.

Pollock would show up that evening, all right, but he was on the wagon. He would not say a word, and would soon go home again. And one person there wasn't a painter at all, as far as we knew. He was a tailor. His name was Isadore Finkelstein, and his shop was right above the tavern. After a couple of drinks, he could talk painting as well as anyone. His grandfather, he said, had been a tailor in Vienna, and had made several suits for the painter Gustav Klimt before the First World War.

And we got on the subject of why, even though we had been given shows which had excited some critics, and which had inspired a big story in *Life* magazine about Pollock, we still weren't making anywhere near enough to live on.

We concluded that it was our clothing and grooming which were holding us back. This was a kind of joke. Everything we said was a kind of joke. I still don't un-

derstand how things got so gruesomely serious for Pollock and Kitchen after only six more years went by.

*　*　*

Slazinger was there, too. That was where I met him.
He was gathering material for a novel about painters—
one of dozens of novels he never wrote.

At the end of that evening, I remember, he said to
me: "I can't get over how passionate you guys are, and
yet so absolutely *unserious.*"

"Everything about life is a joke," I said. "Don't you
know that?"

"No," he said.

*　*　*

Finkelstein declared himself eager to solve the clothing problem of anybody who thought he had one. He
would do it for a small down payment and a manage-
able installment plan. So the next thing I knew, Painters X, Y and Z and I and Kitchen were all upstairs in
Finkelstein's shop, getting measured for suits. Pollock
and Slazinger came along, but only as spectators. Nobody else had any money, so, in character, I made everybody's down payment with the traveler's checks I
had left over from my trip to Florence.

Painters X, Y and Z, incidentally, would pay me back
with pictures the very next afternoon. Painter X had a
key to our apartment, which I had given him after he
was thrown out of his fleabag hotel for setting his bed on
fire. So he and the other two delivered their paintings
and got out again before poor Dorothy could defend
herself.

* * *

Finkelstein the tailor had been a real killer in the war, and so had Kitchen been. I never was.

Finkelstein was a tank gunner in Patton's Third Army. When he measured me for my suit, a suit I still own, he told me, his mouth full of pins, about how a track was blown off his tank by a boy with a rocket launcher two days before the war in Europe ended.

So they shot him before they realized that he was just a boy.

* * *

And here is a surprise: when Finkelstein died of a stroke three years later, when we were all starting to do quite well financially, it turned out that he had been a secret painter all along!

His young widow Rachel, who looked a lot like Circe Berman, now that I think about it, gave him a one-man show in his shop before she closed it up forever. His stuff was unambitious but strong: as representational as he could make it, much like what his fellow war heroes Winston Churchill and Dwight David Eisenhower used to do.

Like them, he enjoyed paint. Like them, he appreciated reality. That was the late painter Isadore Finkelstein.

* * *

After we had been measured for suits we went back down to the tavern for more food and drink and talk, talk, talk, we were joined by a seemingly rich and distinguished gentleman, about sixty years old. I had never seen him before, and neither had any of the others, as nearly as I could tell.

"I hear you are painters," he said. "Do you mind if I just sit here and listen in?" He was between me and Pollock, and across the table from Kitchen.

"Most of us are painters," I said. We weren't about to be rude to him. It was possible that he was an art collector, or maybe on the board of directors of an important museum. We knew what all the critics and dealers looked like. He was much too honest, obviously, to take part in either of those scruffy trades.

"Most of you are painters," he echoed. "Aha! So the simplest thing would be for you to tell me who *isn't* one."

Finkelstein and Slazinger so identified themselves.

"Oh—guessed wrong," he said. He indicated Kitchen. "I wouldn't have thought he was a painter, either," he said, "despite his rough clothes. A musician maybe, or a lawyer or a professional athlete, maybe. A painter? He sure fooled me."

He had to be a clairvoyant, I thought, to home in on the truth about Kitchen with such accuracy! Yes, and he kept his attention locked on Kitchen, as though he were reading his mind. Why would he be more fascinated by somebody who had yet to paint a single interesting picture, than by Pollock, whose work was causing such controversy, and who was sitting right next to him?

He asked Kitchen if he had by any chance seen service in the war.

Kitchen said that he had. He did not elaborate.

"Did that have something to do with your decision to be a painter?" asked the old gentleman.

"No," said Kitchen.

Slazinger would say to me later that he thought that the war had embarrassed Kitchen about how privileged he had always been, easily mastering the piano, easily getting through the best schools, easily beating most people at almost any game, easily getting to be a lieutenant colonel in no time at all, and so on. "To teach himself something about real life," said Slazinger, "he picked one of the few fields where he could not help being a hopeless bungler."

Kitchen said as much to his questioner. "Painting is my Mount Everest," he said. Mount Everest hadn't been climbed yet. That wouldn't happen until 1953, the same year Finkelstein would be buried and have his one-man show.

The old gentleman sat back, seemingly much pleased by this answer.

But then he got much too personal, in my opinion, asking Kitchen if he was independently wealthy, or if his family was supporting him while he made such an arduous climb. I knew that Kitchen would become a very rich man if he outlived his mother and father, and that his parents had refused to give him any money, in the hopes of forcing him to start practicing law or enter politics or take a job on Wall Street, where success was assured.

I didn't think that was any of the old gentleman's business, and I wanted Kitchen to tell him so. But Kitchen told him all—and when he was done answering, his expression indicated that he was ready for another question, no matter what it might be.

This was the next one: "You are married, of course?"

"No," said Kitchen.

"But you *like* women?" said the old gentleman.

He was putting that question to a man who before the end of the war was one of the planet's greatest cocksmen.

"At this point in my life, sir," said Kitchen, "I am a waste of time for women, and women are a waste of time for me."

The old man stood. "I thank you for being so frank and polite with me," he said.

"I try," said Kitchen.

The old gentleman departed. We made guesses as to who and what he might have been. Finkelstein said, I remember, that whoever he was, his clothes had come from England.

* * *

I said I was going to have to borrow or rent a car the next day—to get the house out here ready for my family. I also wanted to have another look at the potato barn I'd rented.

Kitchen asked if he could come along, and I said, "Sure."

And there was this spray rig waiting for him in Montauk. Talk about fate!

* * *

Before we dropped off to sleep on our cots that night, I asked him if he had the least idea who the old gentleman who had questioned him so closely could have been.

"I'll make a really wild guess," he said.

"What is it?" I said.

"I could be wrong, but I think that was my father," he said. "Looked like Dad, sounded like Dad, dressed like

Dad, made wry jokes like Dad. I watched him like a hawk, Rabo, and I said to myself, 'Either this is a very clever imitator, or this is the man who fathered me.' You're smart, and you're my best and only friend. Tell me: if he was simply a good imitator of my father, what could his game have been?"

32

I wound up renting a truck instead of a car for Kitchen's and my fateful foray out here. Talk about Fate: if I hadn't rented a truck, Kitchen might be practicing law now, since there is no way we could have fit the spray rig into a closed sedan, which is the kind of car I would have rented.

Every so often, but not often enough, God knows, I would think of something which would make my wife and family a little less unhappy, and the truck was a case in point. The least I could do was get all the canvases out of our apartment, since they made poor Dorothy feel sick as a dog, even when she was well.

"You're not going to put them in the new house, are you?" she said.

That is what I *had* intended to do. I have never been famous for thinking far ahead. But I said, "No." I formulated a new scheme, which was to put them into the potato barn, but I didn't say so. I hadn't had the nerve to tell her I had rented a potato barn. But she'd found out about it someway. She would find out someway, too, that I had bought myself and Painters X, Y and Z and Kitchen tailor-made suits of the finest materials and workmanship the night before.

"Put them in the potato barn," she said, "and bury them under potatoes. Potatoes we can always use."

* * *

That truck should have been an armored car in a convoy of state police, considering what some of the paintings in there are worth today. I myself considered them valuable, but certainly not *that* valuable. So I could not bring myself to put them in the barn, which was then a musty place, having been home for so long for nothing but potatoes and the earth and bacteria and fungi which so loved to cling to them.

So I rented a dry, clean space under lock and key at Home Sweet Home Moving and Storage out here instead. The rental over the years would absorb a major part of my income. Nor did I overcome my habit of helping painter pals in trouble with whatever cash I had or could lay my hands on, and accepting pictures in return. At least Dorothy did not have to look at the detritus of this habit. Every painting which settled a debt in full went straight from the needy painter's studio to Home Sweet Home.

Her parting words to Kitchen and me when we at last got the pictures out of the apartment were these: "One thing I like about the Hamptons: every so often you see a sign that says 'Town Dump.'"

* * *

If Kitchen had been a perfect Fred Jones to my Dan Gregory, he would have driven the truck. But he was very much the passenger, and I was the chauffeur. He had grown up with chauffeurs, so he didn't think twice when he got in on the passenger side.

I talked about my marriage and the war and the Great Depression, and about how much older Kitchen and I both were, compared with the typical returning veteran. "I should have started a family and settled down years ago," I said. "But how could I have done that when I was the right age to do it? What women did I know anyway?"

"All the returning veterans in the movies are our age or older," he said. That was true. In the movies you seldom saw the babies who had done most of the heavy fighting on the ground in the war.

"Yes—" I said, "and most of the actors in the movies never even went to war. They came home to the wife and kids and swimming pool after every grueling day in front of the cameras, after firing off blank cartridges while men all around them were spitting catsup."

"That's what the young people will think our war was fifty years from now," said Kitchen, "old men and blanks and catsup." So they would. So they do.

"Because of the movies," he predicted, "nobody will believe that it was babies who fought the war."

* * *

"Three years out of our lives," he said about the war.

"You keep forgetting I was a regular," I said. "It was eight years out of mine. And there went my youth, and God, I still want it." Poor Dorothy thought she was marrying a mature, fatherly retired military gentleman. What she got instead was an impossibly self-centered and undisciplined jerk of nineteen or so!

"I can't help it," I said. "My soul knows my meat is doing bad things, and is embarrassed. But my meat just keeps right on doing bad, dumb things."

"Your what and your what?" he said.

"My soul and my meat," I said.

"They're separate?" he said.

"I sure hope they are," I said. I laughed. "I would hate to be responsible for what my meat does."

I told him, only half joking, about how I imagined the soul of each person, myself included, as being a sort of flexible neon tube inside. All the tube could do was receive news about what was happening with the meat, over which it had no control.

"So when people I like do something terrible," I said, "I just flense them and forgive them."

"Flense?" he said. "What's flense?"

"It's what whalers used to do to whale carcasses when they got them on board," I said. "They would strip off the skin and blubber and meat right down to the skeleton. I do that in my head to people—get rid of all the meat so I can see nothing but their souls. Then I forgive them."

"Where would you ever come across a word like *flense?*" he said.

And I said: "In an edition of *Moby Dick* illustrated by
Dan Gregory."

*　*　*

He talked about his father, who is still alive, by the
way, and who has just celebrated his hundredth birth-
day! Think of that.

He adored his father. He also said that he would
never want to compete with him, to try to beat him at
anything. "I would hate that," he said.

"Hate what?" I said.

"To beat him," he said.

He said that the poet Conrad Aiken had lectured at
Yale when Kitchen was in law school there, and had said
that sons of gifted men went into fields occupied by
their fathers, but where their fathers were weak. Aiken's own father had been a great physician and politi-
cian and ladies' man, but had also fancied himself a
poet. "His poetry was no damn good, so Aiken became
a poet," said Kitchen. "I could never do such a thing to
my old man."

*　*　*

What he *would* do to his father six years later, in the
front yard of Kitchen's shack about six miles from here,
was take a shot at him with a pistol. Kitchen was drunk
then, as he often was, and his father had come for the
umpteenth time to beg him to get treatment for his
alcoholism. It can never be proved, but that shot had to
have been intended as a gesture.

When Kitchen saw that he had actually gunned down
his father, with a bullet in the shoulder, it turned out,

nothing would do but that Kitchen put the pistol barrel in his own mouth and kill himself.

It was an accident.

* * *

It was on that fateful truck trip, too, that I got my first look at Edith Taft Fairbanks, who would be my second wife. I had negotiated the rental of the barn from her husband, who was an affable idler, who seemed a useless, harmless waster of life to me back then, but who would become the role model I kept in mind when he died and I became her husband.

Prophetically, she was carrying a tamed raccoon in her arms. She was a magical tamer of almost any sort of animal, an overwhelmingly loving and uncritical nurturer of anything and everything that looked half alive. That's what she would do to me when I was living as a hermit in the barn and she needed a new husband: she tamed me with nature poems and good things to eat which she left outside my sliding doors. I'm sure she tamed her first husband, too, and thought of him lovingly and patronizingly as some kind of dumb animal.

She never said what kind of animal she thought he was. I know what kind of animal she thought *I* was, because she came right out and said it to a female relative from Cincinnati at our wedding reception, when I was all dressed up in my Izzy Finkelstein suit: "I want you to meet my tamed raccoon."

* * *

I will be *buried* in that suit, too. It says so in my will: "I am to be buried next to my wife Edith in Green River Cemetery in the dark blue suit whose label says: 'Made

to order for Rabo Karabekian by Isadore Finkelstein.' "
It wears and wears.

* * *

Well—the execution of that will still lies in the future,
but just about everything else has vanished into the
past, including Circe Berman. She finished up her book
and returned to Baltimore two weeks ago.

On her last night here, she wanted me to take her
dancing, and I again refused. I took her to supper at the
American Hotel in Sag Harbor instead. Just another
tourist trap nowadays, Sag Harbor used to be a whaling
port. You can still see the mansions of the brave captains
who sailed from there to the Pacific Ocean, around the
tip of South America, and then came home millionaires.

In the lobby of the hotel is a guest register opened to
a date at the peak of the whale-killing industry, so dis-
reputable nowadays: March 1, 1849. Back then, Circe's
ancestors were in the Russian Empire and mine in the
Turkish Empire, which would have made them enemies.

We feasted on lobsters, and drank in moderation in
order to become voluble. It is a bad thing to need a
drink, everybody is saying now, and I in fact went without alcohol the whole time I was a hermit. But my
feelings about Mrs. Berman on the eve of her departure
were so contradictory that, without a drink, I might
have eaten in wooden silence. But I certainly wasn't
going to drive with a couple of drinks in me, and neither was she. It used to be almost fashionable to drive
when drunk, but no more, no more.

So I hired a boyfriend of Celeste's to drive us over
there in his father's car, and then pick us up again.

*   *   *

In the simplest terms: I was sorry that she was leaving, because she was exciting to have around. But she could also be too exciting, telling everybody exactly what to do. So I was also glad that she was going, since what I wanted most, with my own book so nearly finished, was peace and quiet for a change. To put it another way: we were acquaintances, despite our months together. We had not become great friends.

That would change, however, once I had shown her what was in the potato barn.

Yes, that's right: this determined widow from Baltimore, before she left, persuaded this old Armenian geezer to unlock the locks and turn on the floodlights in the potato barn.

What did I get in exchange? I think we're really friends now.

33

When we got home from the American Hotel, the first thing she said was: "One thing you don't have to worry about: I'm not going to badger you about the keys to the potato barn."

"Thank God!" I said.

I think she was certain right then that, before the night was over, one way or another, she was damn well going to see what was in the potato barn.

"I only want you to draw me a picture," she said.

"Do what?" I said.

"You're a very modest man—" she said, "to the point where anybody who believed you would think you were no good at anything."

"Except camouflage," I said. "You're forgetting camouflage. I was awarded a Presidential Unit Citation, my platoon was so good at camouflage."

"O.K.—camouflage," she said.

"We were so good at camouflage," I said, "that half the things we hid from the enemy have to this very day never been seen again!"

"And that's not true," she said.

"We're having a celebration, so all sorts of things have been said which are not true," I said. "That's how to act at a party."

* * *

"You want me to go home to Baltimore knowing a whole lot of things about you which are not true?" she said.

"Everything that's true about me you should have learned before now, given your profound powers of investigation," I said. "This is just a party."

"I still don't know whether you can really draw or not," she said.

"Don't worry about it," I said.

"That's the bedrock of your life, to hear you tell it," she said. "That and camouflage. You were no good as a commercial artist, and you were no good as a serious artist, and you were no good as a husband or a father, and your great collection of paintings is an accident. But you keep coming back to one thing you're proud of: you could really draw."

"It's true," I said. "I didn't realize that, but now that you mention it, it's true."

"So prove it," she said.

"It's a very small boast," I said. "I wasn't an Albrecht

Dürer. I could draw better than you or Slazinger or the cook—or Pollock or Terry Kitchen. I was born with this gift which certainly doesn't look like much when you compare me with all the far superior draughtsmen who've lived and died. I wowed the grade school and then the high school in San Ignacio, California. If I'd lived ten thousand years ago, I might have wowed the cave dwellers of Lascaux, France—whose standards for draughtsmanship must have been on about the same level as those of San Ignacio."

* * *

"If your book is actually published," she said, "you're going to have to include at least one picture that proves you can draw. Readers will insist on that."

"Poor souls," I said. "And the worst thing about getting as old as I am—"

"You're not that old," she said.

"Old enough!" I said. "And the worst thing is that you keep finding yourself in the middle of the same old conversations, no matter who you're talking to. Slazinger didn't think I could draw. My first wife didn't think I could draw. My second wife didn't care whether I could or not. I was just an old raccoon she brought in from the barn and turned into a house pet. She loved animals whether they could draw or not."

* * *

"What did you say to your first wife when she bet you couldn't draw?" she said.

"We had just moved out in the country where she didn't know a soul," I said. "There still wasn't heat in the house, and I was trying to keep us warm with fires in the three fireplaces—like my pioneer ancestors. And Dorothy was finally trying to catch up on art, reading up on it, since she had resigned herself to being stuck with an artist. She had never seen me draw—because not drawing and forgetting everything I knew about art, I thought, was the magic key to my becoming a serious painter.

"So, sitting in front of a fire in the kitchen fireplace, with all the heat going up the flue instead of coming out in the room," I said, "Dorothy read in an art magazine what an Italian sculptor had said about the first Abstract Expressionist paintings ever to be shown in a major show in Europe—at the Venice Biennale in 1950, the same year I had my reunion with Marilee."

"You had a painting there?" said Circe.

"No," I said. "It was just Gorky and Pollock and de Kooning. And this Italian sculptor, who was supposedly very important back then, but who is all but forgotten now, said this about what we thought we were up to: 'These Americans are very interesting. They dive into the water before they learn to swim.' He meant we couldn't draw.

"Dorothy picked up on that right away. She wanted to hurt me as much as I had hurt her, so she said, 'So that's it! You guys all paint the way you do because you couldn't paint something real if you *had* to.'

"I didn't rebut her with words. I snatched a green crayon Dorothy had been using to make a list of all the things inside and outside the house that had to be repaired, and I drew portraits on the kitchen wall of our two boys, who were asleep in front of the fireplace in the living room. I just did their heads—life size. I didn't even go into the living room to look at them first. The wall was new Sheetrock which I had nailed over the cracked plaster. I hadn't got around to filling and taping the joints between the sheets yet, and covering the nailheads. I never would.

"Dorothy was flabbergasted," I said to Circe. "She said to me: 'Why don't you do that all the time?' And I said to her, and this was the first time I ever said 'fuck' to her, no matter how angry we might have been with each other: 'It's just too fucking *easy*.' "

*   *   *

"You never did fill in the joints between the Sheetrock?" said Mrs. Berman.

"That is certainly a woman's question," I said. "And my manly answer is this one: 'No, I did not.' "

"So what happened to the portraits?" she said. "Were they painted over?"

"No," I said. "They stayed there on the Sheetrock for six years. But then I came home half drunk one afternoon, and found my wife and children and the pictures gone, and a note from Dorothy saying they were gone forever. She had cut the pictures out of the Sheetrock and taken them with her. There were two big square holes where the pictures used to be."

"You must have felt awful," said Mrs. Berman.

"Yes," I said. "Pollock and Kitchen had killed themselves only a few weeks before that, and my own paintings were falling apart. So when I saw those two squares cut out of the Sheetrock in that empty house—" I stopped. "Never mind," I said.

"Finish the sentence, Rabo," she begged.

"That was as close as I'll ever be," I said, "to feeling what my father must have felt when he was a young teacher—and found himself all alone in his village after the massacre."

* * *

Slazinger was another one who had never seen me draw, who wondered if I could really draw. I had been living out here for a couple of years by then, and he came by to watch me paint in the potato barn. I had set up a stretched and primed canvas eight by eight feet, and was about to lay on a coat of Sateen Dura-Luxe with a roller. It was a shade of greenish burnt orange called "Hungarian Rhapsody." Little did I know that Dorothy, back at the house, was slathering our whole bedroom with "Hungarian Rhapsody." But that is another story.

"Tell me, Rabo—" said Slazinger, "if I put on that same paint with that same roller, would the picture still be a Karabekian?"

"Absolutely," I said, "provided you have in reserve what Karabekian has in reserve."

"Like what?" he said.

"Like this," I said. There was dust in a pothole in the floor, and I picked up some of it on the balls of both my thumbs. Working both thumbs simultaneously, I sketched a caricature of Slazinger's face on the canvas in thirty seconds.

"Jesus!" he said. "I had no idea you could draw like that!"

"You're looking at a man who has *options,*" I said.

And he said: "I guess you do, I guess you *do.*"

* * *

I covered up that caricature with a couple of coats of "Hungarian Rhapsody," and laid on tapes which were supposed to be pure abstraction, but which to me were secretly six deer in a forest glade. The deer were near the left edge. On the right was a red vertical band, which to me, again secretly, was the soul of a hunter drawing a bead on one of them. I called it "Hungarian Rhapsody Number Six," which was bought by the Guggenheim Museum.

That picture was in storage when it started to fall apart like all the rest of them. A woman curator just happened to walk by and see all this tape and flakes of Sateen Dura-Luxe on the floor, so she called me up to ask what could be done to restore the picture, and whether they might be at fault someway. I didn't know where she had been the past year, when my pictures had become notorious for falling apart everywhere. She honestly thought maybe the Guggenheim hadn't provided proper humidity controls or whatever. I was at that time living like an animal in the potato barn, friendless and unloved. But I did have a telephone.

"One very strange thing—" she went on, "this big face has emerged from the canvas." It was the caricature, of course, which I had drawn with filthy thumbs.

"You should notify the Pope," I said.

"The Pope?" she said.

"Yes," I said. "You may have the next best thing to the *Shroud of Turin*."

I had better explain to young readers that the *Shroud of Turin* is a linen sheet in which a dead person has been wrapped, which bears the imprint of an adult male who has been crucified, which the best scientists of today agree may indeed be two thousand years old. It is widely believed to have swaddled none other than

Jesus Christ, and is the chief treasure of the Cathedral of San Giovanni Battista in Turin, Italy.

My joke with the lady at the Guggenheim suggested that it might be the face of Jesus emerging from the canvas—possibly just in time to prevent World War Three.

But she topped my joke. She said, "Well—I would call the Pope right away, except for one thing."

"What's that?" I said.

And she said: "You happen to be talking to somebody who used to date Paul Slazinger."

*   *   *

I made her the same offer I had made everybody else: that I would duplicate the painting exactly in more durable materials, paints and tapes which really *would* outlive the smile on the "Mona Lisa."

But the Guggenheim, like everybody else, turned me down. Nobody wanted to spoil the hilarious footnote I had become in art history. With a little luck, my last name might actually find its way into dictionaries:

kar•a•bek•i•an (ˌkar-a-'bek-ē-an), n. (from Rabo Karabekian, U.S. 20th cent. painter). Fiasco in which a person causes total destruction of own work and reputation through stupidity, carelessness or both.

34

When I refused to draw a pic-
ture for Mrs. Berman, she said, "Oh—you are such a
stubborn little boy!"

"I am a stubborn little old *gentleman*," I said, "clinging to his dignity and self-respect as best he can."

"Just tell me what *kind* of thing it is in the barn—"
she wheedled, "animal, vegetable or mineral?"

"All three," I said.

"How big?" she said.

I told her the truth: "Eight feet high and sixty-four
feet long."

"You're kidding me again," she surmised.

"Of course," I said.

Out in the barn were eight panels of primed and stretched canvas placed side by side, each one eight feet by eight feet. They formed, as I had told her, a continuous surface sixty-four feet long. They were held upright in back by two-by-fours, and ran like a fence down the middle of the potato barn. These were the same panels which had shed the paint and tape of what had been my most famous and then most infamous creation, the picture which had graced and then disgraced the lobby of the GEFFCo headquarters on Park Avenue: "Windsor Blue Number Seventeen."

* * *

Here is how they came back into my possession, three months before dear Edith died:

They were found entombed in a locked chamber in the bottommost of the three basement floors under the Matsumoto Building, formerly the GEFFCo Building. They were recognized for what they were, with shreds of Sateen Dura-Luxe clinging to them here and there, by an inspector from Matsumoto's insurance company, who was looking for fire hazards deep underground. There was a locked steel door, and nobody had any idea what was on the other side.

The inspector got permission to break in. This was a woman and, as she told me on the telephone: she was the first female safety inspector for her company, and also the first black. "I am two birds with one stone," she said, and she laughed. She had a very nice laugh. There was no malice or mockery in it. In offering to return my canvases to me after all those years, with the absent-minded approval of Matsumoto, she was simply expressing her reluctance to see anything go to waste.

"I'm the only one who cares one way or another," she said, "so *you* tell me what to do. You'd have to pick them up yourself," she said.

"How did you know what they *were*?" I said.

She had been a prenursing student at Skidmore College, she said, and had taken, as one of her precious few electives, a course in art appreciation. She was a registered nurse like my first wife Dorothy, but had given up that profession because doctors, she said, treated her like an idiot and a slave. Also: the hours were long and the pay was low, and she had an orphaned niece to support and keep company.

Her art appreciation teacher showed slides of famous pictures, and two of these were of "Windsor Blue Number Seventeen," before and after it fell apart.

"How can I thank him?" I said.

"I think he was trying to lighten up the course," she said. "The rest of it was so *serious*."

*　*　*

"Do you want the canvases or not?" she said. There was a long silence, so she finally said, "Hello? Hello?"

"Sorry," I said. "That may seem like a simple question to you, but it's a biggie to me. To me it's as though you called me up out of the blue on a day like any other day, and asked me if I was grown up yet."

If harmless objects like those rectangles of stretched canvas were hobgoblins to me, could fill me with shame, yes, with rage at a world which had entrapped me into being a failure and a laughingstock and so on, then I *wasn't* a grown-up yet, although I was then sixty-eight years old.

"So what is your answer?" she said on the telephone.

"I'm waiting myself to hear it," I said. I had no use for the canvases—or so I thought back then. I honestly never expected to paint again. Storing them would be no problem, since there was plenty of space in the potato barn. Could I sleep well here with the worst of the embarrassments from my past right here on the property? I hoped so.

I heard myself say this at last: "Please—don't throw them away. I will call Home Sweet Home Moving and Storage out here, and have them picked up as soon as possible. Please tell me your name again—so they can ask for you."

And she said this: "Mona Lisa Trippingham."

* * *

When GEFFCo hung "Windsor Blue Number Seventeen" in its lobby, with fanfare about such an old company's keeping on top of the latest developments not only in technology but in the arts, the company's publicity people hoped to say that "Windsor Blue Number Seventeen" was superlative in terms of size—if not the largest painting in the world, then at least the largest painting in New York City, or whatever. But there were several murals right in the city, and God knows in the world, which easily exceeded my painting's 512 square feet.

The publicity people wondered if it might not be a record holder for a painting *hung on a wall*—ignoring the fact that it was in fact eight separate panels, mated in back with C-clamps. But that wouldn't do, either, since it turned out that the Museum of the City of New York had three *continuous* paintings on canvas, *stitched* together to be sure, as high as mine and a third again as long! They were curious artifacts—an early effort at making movies, you might say, since they had rollers at either end. They could be unwound from one and rewound on the other. An audience could see only a small part of the whole at any time. These Brobdingnagian ribbons were decorated with mountains and rivers and virgin forests and limitless grasslands on which buffalo grazed, and deserts where diamonds or rubies or gold nuggets might be had for the stooping. These were the United States of America.

Lecturers traveled all over Northern Europe with such pictures in olden times. With assistants to unroll one end and roll up the other, they urged all ambitious and able persons to abandon tired old Europe and lay claim to rich and beautiful properties in the Promised Land, which were practically theirs for the asking.

Why should a real man stay home when he could be raping a virgin continent?

* * *

I had the eight panels purged of every trace of faithless Sateen Dura-Luxes, and restretched and reprimed. I had them set up in the barn, dazzling white in their restored virginity, just as they had been before I transmuted them into "Windsor Blue Number Seventeen."

I explained to my wife that this eccentric project was an exorcism of an unhappy past, a symbolic repairing of all the damage I had done to myself and others during my brief career as a painter. That was yet another instance, though, of putting into words what could not be put into words: why and how a painting had come to be.

The long and narrow barn, a century old, was as much a part of it as all that white, white, white.

The powerful floodlights dangling from tracks on the ceiling were part of it, pouring megawatts of energy into all that white sizing, making it far whiter than I would have believed white could ever be. I had caused those artificial suns to be installed when I received the commission to create "Windsor Blue Number Seventeen."

"What are you going to do with it next?" dear Edith asked.

"It's done," I said.

"Are you going to sign it?" she said.

"That would spoil it," I replied. "A flyspeck would spoil it."

"Does it have a title?" she said.

"Yes," I said, and I gave it a title on the spot, one as long as the title Paul Slazinger had given his book on successful revolutions: "I Tried and Failed and Cleaned Up Afterwards, so It's *Your* Turn Now."

* * *

I had my own death in mind—and what people would say about me afterwards. That was when I first locked up the barn, but with only a single padlock and hasp. I assumed, as my father had and as most husbands do, that I would of course be the first of our pair to die. So I had whimsically self-pitying instructions for Edith as to what she was to do immediately following my burial.

"Hold my wake in the barn, Edith," I said, "and when

people ask you about all the white, white, white, you tell them that it was your husband's last painting, even though he didn't paint it. And then you tell them what the title is."

*   *   *

But she died first, and only two months after that. Her heart stopped, and down she fell into a flower bed.

"No pain," the doctor said.

At her burial at noon in Green River Cemetery, in a grave only a few yards from those of the other two Musketeers, Jackson Pollock and Terry Kitchen, I had my strongest vision yet of human souls unencumbered, unembarrassed by their unruly meat. There was this rectangular hole in the ground, and standing around it were all these pure and innocent neon tubes.

Was I crazy? You bet.

Her wake was in the home of a friend of hers, not mine, a mile up the beach from here. The husband did not attend!

Nor did he reenter this house, where he had been so useless and contented and loved without reason for one third of his life and one quarter of the twentieth century.

He went out to the barn, unlocked the sliding doors and turned on the lights. He stared at all that white.

Then he got into his Mercedes and drove to a hardware store in East Hampton, which carried art supplies. I bought everything a painter could ever wish for, save for the ingredient he himself would have to supply: soul, soul, soul.

The clerk was new to the area, and so did not know who I was. He saw a nameless old man in a shirt and tie and a suit made to order by Izzy Finkelstein—and a patch over one eye. The cyclops was in a high state of agitation.

"You're a painter, are you, sir?" said the clerk. He was perhaps twenty years old. He hadn't even been born when I stopped painting, stopped making pictures of any kind.

I spoke one word to him before leaving. This was it: "Renaissance."

* * *

The servants quit. I had become an untamed old raccoon again, who spent all his life in and around the potato barn. I kept the sliding doors closed, so that nobody could see what it was that I did in there. I did it for six months!

When I was done, I bought five more locks and hasps for the sliding doors, and snapped them shut. I hired new servants, and had a lawyer draw up a new will, which stipulated, as I have said, that I be buried in my Izzy Finkelstein suit, that all I owned was to go to my two sons, provided that they did a certain thing in memory of their Armenian ancestors, and that the barn was not to be unlocked until after my burial.

My sons have done quite well in the world, despite the horrors of their childhood. As I've said, their last name now is that of their good stepfather. Henri Steel is a civilian contract compliance officer at the Pentagon. Terry Steel is a publicity man for the Chicago Bears, which, since I own a piece of the Cincinnati Bengals, makes us sort of a football family.

* * *

Having done all that, I found I was able to take up residence in this house again, to hire new servants, and to become the empty and peaceful old man to whom Circe Berman addressed this question on the beach four months ago: "Tell me how your parents died."

On her last night in the Hamptons, she now said to me: "Animal, vegetable *and* mineral? All three?"

"Word of honor," I said. "All three, all three." With colors and binders taken from creatures and plants and the ground beneath us, every painting was surely all three, all three.

"Why won't you show it to me?" she said.

"Because it is the last thing I have to give to the world," I said. "I don't want to be around when people say whether it is any good or not."

"Then you are a coward," she said, "and that is how I will remember you."

I thought that over, and then I heard myself say: "All right, I will go get the keys. And then, Mrs. Berman, I would be most grateful if you would come with me."

*   *   *

Out into the dark we went, a flashlight beam dancing before us. She was subdued, humble, awed and virginal. I was elated, high as a kite and absolutely petrified.

We walked on flagstones at first, but then they veered off in the direction of the carriage house. After that we trod the stubble path cut through the wilderness by Franklin Cooley and his mowing machine.

I unlocked the barn doors and reached inside, my fingers on the light switch. "Scared?" I said.

"Yes," she said.

"So am I," I said.

Remember now: we were standing at the extreme right end of a painting eight feet high and sixty-four feet long. When I turned on the floodlights, we would be seeing the picture compressed by foreshortening to a seeming triangle eight feet high, all right, but only five feet wide. There was no telling from that vantage point what the painting really was—what the painting was all *about.*

I flicked on the switch.

There was a moment of silence, and then Mrs. Berman gasped in wonderment.

"Stay right where you are," I told her, "and tell me what you think of it."

"I can't come any farther?" she said.

"In a minute," I said, "but first I want to hear you say what it looks like from here."

"A big fence," she said.

"Go on," I said.

"A very big fence, an incredibly high and long fence," she said, "every square inch of it encrusted with the most gorgeous jewelry."

"Thank you very much," I said. "And now take my hand and close your eyes. I am going to lead you to the middle, and you can look again."

She closed her eyes, and she followed me as unresistingly as a toy balloon.

When we were in the middle, with thirty-two feet of the painting extending to either side, I told her to open her eyes again.

We were standing on the rim of a beautiful green valley in the springtime. By actual count, there were five thousand, two hundred and nineteen people on the rim with us or down below. The largest person was the size of a cigarette, and the smallest a flyspeck. There were farmhouses here and there, and the ruins of a medieval watchtower on the rim where we stood. The picture was so realistic that it might have been a photograph.

"Where are we?" said Circe Berman.

"Where I was," I said, "when the sun came up the day the Second World War ended in Europe."

35

It is all part of the regular tour of my museum now. First come the doomed little girls on swings in the foyer, and then the earliest works of the first Abstract Expressionists, and then the perfectly tremendous whatchamacallit in the potato barn. I have unspiked the sliding doors at the far end of the barn, so that the greatly increased flow of visitors can move past the whatchamacallit without eddies and backwash. In one end they go, and out the other. Many of them will go through two times or more: not the whole show, just through the potato barn.

Ha!

No solemn critic has yet appeared. Several laymen and laywomen have asked me, however, to say what sort of a painting I would call it. I told them what I will tell the first critic to show up, if one ever comes, and one may never come, since the whatchamacallit is so exciting to the common people:

"It isn't a painting at all! It's a tourist attraction! It's a World's Fair! It's a Disneyland!"

* * *

It is a gruesome Disneyland. Nobody is cute there.

On an average, there are ten clearly drawn World War Two survivors to each square foot of the painting. Even the figures in the distance, no bigger than fly-specks, when examined through one of several magnifying glasses I keep in the barn, prove to be concentration-camp victims or slave laborers or prisoners of war from this or that country, or soldiers from this or that military unit on the German side, or local farmers and their families, or lunatics set free from asylums, and on and on.

There is a war story to go with every figure in the picture, no matter how small. I made up a story, and then painted the person it had happened to. I at first made myself available in the barn to tell anyone who asked what the story was of this person or that one, but soon gave up in exhaustion. "Make up your own war stories as you look at the whatchamacallit," I tell people. I stay in the house here, and simply point the way out to the potato barn.

* * *

That night with Circe Berman, though, I was glad to tell her any of the stories she wished to hear.

"Are you in there?" she said.

I pointed out myself at the bottom and right above the floor. I pointed with the toe of my shoe. I was the largest figure—the one as big as a cigarette. I was also the only one of the thousands with his back to the camera, so to speak. The crack between the fourth and fifth panels ran up my spine and parted my hair, and might be taken for the soul of Rabo Karabekian.

"This man clinging to your leg is looking up at you as though you were God," she said.

"He is dying of pneumonia, and will be dead in two hours," I said. "He is a Canadian bombardier who was shot down over an oil field in Hungary. He doesn't know who I am. He can't even see my face. All he can see is a thick fog which isn't there, and he's asking me if we are home yet."

"And what are you telling him?" she said.

"What would *you* tell him?" I said. "I'm telling him, 'Yes! We're home! We're home!' "

"Who is this man in the funny-looking suit?" she said.

"That is a concentration-camp guard who threw away his SS uniform and stole the suit from a scarecrow," I said. I pointed out a group of concentration camp victims far away from the masquerading guard. Several of them were on the ground and dying, like the Canadian bombardier. "He brought these people to the valley and dumped them, but doesn't know where to go next. Anybody who catches him will know he is an SS man—because he has his serial number tattooed on his upper left arm."

"And these two?" she said.

"Yugoslavian partisans," I said.

"This one?" she said.

"A sergeant major in the Moroccan Spahis, captured in North Africa," I said.

"And this one with a pipe in his mouth?" she said.

"A Scottish glider pilot captured on D-Day," I said.

"They're just from everywhere, aren't they?" she said.

"This is a Gurkha here," I said, "all the way from Nepal. And this machine-gun squad in German uniforms: they're Ukrainians who changed sides early in the war. When the Russians finally reach the valley, they'll be hanged or shot."

"There don't seem to be any women," she said.

"Look closer," I said. "Half the concentration camp people and half the people from the lunatic asylums are women. They just don't look much like women anymore. They aren't what you might call 'movie stars.'"

"There don't seem to be any *healthy* women," she said.

"Wrong again," I said. "You'll find healthy ones at either end—in the corners at the bottom."

We went to the extreme right end for a look. "My goodness," she said, "it's like a display in a museum of natural history." So it was. There was a farmhouse down at the bottom of both ends: each one buttoned up tight like a little fort, its high gates closed, and all the animals in the courtyard. And I had made a schematic cut through the earth below them, so as to show their cellars, too, just as a museum display might give away the secrets of animals' burrows underground.

"The healthy women are in the cellar with the beets and potatoes and turnips," I said. "They are putting off being raped as long as possible, but they have heard the history of other wars in the area, so they know that rape will surely come."

"Does the picture have a title?" she said, rejoining me at the middle.

"Yes it does," I said.

"What is it?" she said.

And I said: " 'Now It's the Women's Turn.' "

*   *   *

"Am I crazy," she said, indicating a figure lurking near the ruined watchtower, "or is this a Japanese soldier?"

"That's what he is," I said. "He is a major in the army. You can tell that from the gold star and two brown stripes on the cuff of his left sleeve. And he still has his sword. He would rather die than give up his sword."

"I'm surprised that there were any Japanese there," she said.

"There weren't," I said, "but I thought there should be one there so I put one there."

"Why?" she said.

"Because," I said, "the Japanese were as responsible as the Germans for turning Americans into a bunch of bankrupt militaristic fuckups—after we'd done such a good job of being sincere war-haters after the First World War."

"And this woman lying here—" she said, "she's dead?"

"She's dead," I said. "She's an old queen of the Gypsies."

"She's so fat," she said. "Is she the only fat person? Everybody else is so skinny."

"Dying is the only way to get fat in Happy Valley," I said. "She's as fat as a circus freak because she's been dead three days."

" 'Happy Valley,' " echoed Circe.

"Or 'Peacetime' or 'Heaven' or 'the Garden of Eden' or 'Springtime' or whatever you want to call it," I said.

"She's the only one who's all alone," said Circe. "Or is she?"

"Just about," I said. "People don't smell too nice after they've been dead three days. She was the first stranger to arrive in Happy Valley, and she came all alone, and she died almost right away."

"Where are the other Gypsies?" she said.

"With their fiddles and tambourines and brightly painted caravans?" I said. "And their reputation for thieving, which was much deserved?"

* * *

Mrs. Berman told me a legend about Gypsies I had never heard before: "They stole the nails from the Roman soldiers who were about to crucify Jesus," she said. "When the soldiers looked for the nails, they had disappeared mysteriously. Gypsies had stolen them, and Jesus and the crowd had to wait until the soldiers sent for new nails. After that, God Almighty gave permission to all Gypsies to steal all they could." She pointed to the bloated Gypsy queen. "She believed that story. All Gypsies do."

"Too bad for her that she believed it," I said. "Or maybe it didn't matter whether she believed it or not, since she was starving to death when she arrived all alone in Happy Valley.

"She tried to steal a chicken from the farmhouse," I

said. "The farmer saw her from this bedroom window, and took a shot at her with a small-caliber rifle he kept under his feather mattress. She ran away. He thought he had missed her, but he hadn't. She had a little bullet in her abdomen, and she lay down there and died. Three days later, the rest of us came along."

*   *   *

"If she's a queen of the Gypsies, where are her subjects?" Circe asked again.

I explained that she had been queen of only about forty people at the peak of her power, including babes in arms. While there were notorious disputes in Europe as to which races and subraces were vermin, all Europeans could agree that the thieving, fortune-telling, child-stealing Gypsies were the enemies of all decent humankind. So they were hunted down everywhere. The queen and her people gave up their caravans, and their traditional costumes, too—gave up everything which might identify them as Gypsies. They hid in forests in the daytime, and foraged for food at night.

One night, when the queen went out alone to look for food, one of her subjects, a fourteen-year-old boy, was caught stealing a ham from a Slovak mortar squad which had deserted the German lines on the Russian front. They were headed home, which wasn't far from Happy Valley. They made the boy lead them to the Gypsy camp, where they killed everybody. So when the queen came back, she didn't have any subjects.

Such was the story I made up for Circe Berman.

*   *   *

Circe provided the missing link in the narrative. "So she wandered into Happy Valley, looking for other Gypsies," she said.

"Right!" I said. "But there weren't many Gypsies to be found anywhere in Europe. Most of them had been rounded up and gassed in extermination camps, which was fine with everybody. Who likes thieves?"

She took a closer look at the dead woman and turned away in disgust. "Ugh!" she said. "What's coming from her mouth? Blood and maggots?"

"Rubies and diamonds," I said. "She smells so awful, and looks like such bad luck, that nobody has come close enough to notice yet."

"And of all these people here," she said wonderingly, "who will be the first to notice?"

I indicated the former concentration camp guard in the rags of a scarecrow. "This man," I said.

36

"Soldiers, soldiers, soldiers," she marveled. "Uniforms, uniforms, uniforms."

The uniforms, what was left of them, were as authentic as I could make them. That was my homage to my master, Dan Gregory.

"Fathers are always so proud, the first time they see their sons in uniform," she said.

"I know Big John Karpinski was," I said. He is my neighbor to the north, of course. Big John's son Little John did badly in high school, and the police caught him selling dope. So he joined the Army while the Vietnam War was going on. And the first time he came

home in uniform, I never saw Big John so happy, because it looked to him as though Little John was all
straightened out and would finally amount to something.

But then Little John came home in a body bag.

* * *

Big John and his wife Dorene, incidentally, are dividing their farm, where three generations of Karpinskis
grew up, into six-acre lots. It was in the local paper
yesterday. Those lots will sell like hotcakes, since so
many of the second-story windows of houses built on
them, overlooking my property, will have a water view.

Big John and Dorene will become cash millionaires in
a condominium in Florida, where winter never comes.
So they are losing their own sacred plot of earth at the
foot of their own Mount Ararat, so to speak—without
experiencing that ultimate disgrace: a massacre.

"Was *your* father proud of you when he saw *you* for
the first time in a uniform?" Circe asked me.

"He didn't live to see it," I said, "and I'm glad he
didn't. If he had, he would have thrown an awl or a boot
at me."

"Why?" she said.

"Don't forget that it was young soldiers whose parents thought they were finally going to amount to
something who killed everybody he'd ever known and
loved. If he'd seen me in a uniform, he would have
bared his teeth like a dog with rabies. He would have
said, 'Swine!' He would have said, 'Pig!' He would have
said, 'Murderer! Get out of here!' "

* * *

"What do you think will eventually become of this painting?" she said.

"It's too big to throw away," I said. "Maybe it'll go to that private museum in Lubbock, Texas, where they have most of the paintings of Dan Gregory. I thought it might wind up behind the longest bar in the world, wherever that is—probably in Texas, too. But the customers would be climbing up on the bar all the time, trying to see what was really going on—kicking over glasses, stepping on the complimentary hors d'oeuvres."

I said that it would eventually be up to my two sons, Terry and Henri, to decide what was to become of "Now It's the Women's Turn."

"You're leaving it to *them?*" she said. She knew that they hated me, and had had their last name legally changed to that of Dorothy's second husband, Roy—the only *real* father they'd ever had.

"You think it's kind of a *joke* to leave them this?" said Circe. "You think it's worthless? I'm here to tell you this is a *terribly* important painting *some*way."

"I think maybe it's terribly important the same way a head-on collision is important," I said. "There's undeniable impact. Something has sure as hell happened."

"You leave those ingrates this," she said, "and you'll make them multimillionaires."

"They'll be that in any case," I said. "I'm leaving them everything I own, including your pictures of the little girls in swings and the pool table, unless you want those back. After I die, they'll have to do only one little thing to get it all."

"What's that?" she said.

"Merely have their names and those of my grandchildren legally changed back to 'Karabekian,' " I said.

"You care that much?" she said.

"I'm doing it for my mother," I said. "She wasn't even a Karabekian by birth, but she was the one who wanted, no matter where, no matter what, the name Karabekian to live on and on."

* * *

"How many of these are portraits of actual people?" she said.

"The bombardier clinging to my leg: that's his face, as I remember it. These two Estonians in German uniforms are Laurel and Hardy. This French collaborator here is Charlie Chaplin. These two Polish slave laborers on the other side of the tower from me are Jackson Pollock and Terry Kitchen."

"So there you are across the bottom: the Three Musketeers," she said.

"There we are," I agreed.

"The death of the other two so close together must have been a terrible blow to you," she said.

"We'd stopped being friends long before then," I said. "It was all the boozing we did together that made people call us that. It didn't have anything to do with painting. We could have been plumbers. One or the other of us would stop drinking for a little while, and sometimes all three of us—and that was that for the Three Musketeers, long before the other two killed themselves. 'Quite a blow,' you say, Mrs. Berman? Not at all. The only thing I did after I heard about it was become a hermit for eight years or so."

* * *

"And then Rothko killed himself after that," she said.

"Yup," I said. We were extricating ourselves from Happy Valley, and returning to real life. The melancholy roll-call of real-life suicides among the Abstract Expressionists again: Gorky by hanging in 1948, Pollock and then almost immediately Kitchen, by drunken driving and then pistol in 1956—and then Rothko with all possible messiness by knife in 1970.

I told her with sharpness which surprised me, and surprised her, too, that those violent deaths were like our drinking, and had nothing to do with our painting.

"I certainly won't argue with you," she said.

"Really!" I said. "Word of honor!" I said, my vehemence unspent. "The whole magical thing about our painting, Mrs. Berman, and this was old stuff in music, but it was brand new in painting: it was pure *essence of human wonder*, and wholly apart from food, from sex, from clothes, from houses, from drugs, from cars, from news, from money, from crime, from punishment, from games, from war, from peace—and surely apart from the universal human impulse among painters and plumbers alike toward inexplicable despair and self-destruction!"

* * *

"You know how old I was when you were standing on the rim of this valley?" she said.

"No," I said.

"One year old," she said. "And I don't mean to be rude, Rabo, but this picture is so rich, I don't think I can look at it any more tonight."

"I understand," I said. We had been out there for two hours. I myself was all worn out, but also twangingly proud and satisfied.

*　*　*

So there we were back in the doorway again, and I had my hand on the light switch. Since there were no stars that night, and no moon, a flick of that switch would plunge us into total darkness.

She asked me this: "Is there anything anywhere in the picture which says when and where this happened?"

"Nothing to say *where* it was," I said. "There's one place that says *when* it was, but that's at the other end and way up high. If you really want to see it, I'll have to get not only a stepladder but a magnifying glass."

"Some other time," she said.

I described it for her. "There's this Maori, a corporal in the New Zealand Field Artillery who was captured in a battle outside Tobruk, Libya. I'm sure you know who the Maoris are," I said.

"They're Polynesians," she said. "They're the aborigines of New Zealand."

"Exactly!" I said. "They were cannibals and were divided into many warring tribes until the white man came. So this Polynesian is sitting on a discarded German ammunition box. There are three bullets still in the bottom of it, in case anybody needs one. He is trying to read what is an inside page from a newspaper. He has grabbed it as it scuttled across the valley in the breeze that came with sunrise."

I went on, my fingertips touching the light switch: "The page is from an anti-Semitic weekly published in

Riga, Latvia, during the German occupation of that little country. It is six months old, and offers tips on gardening and home canning. The Maori is studying it very earnestly, in the hopes of leaning what we would all like to know about ourselves: where he is, what is going on, and what is likely to happen next.

"If we had a stepladder and a magnifying glass, Mrs. Berman, you could see for yourself that written in tiny characters on the ammunition box is this date, when you were only one year old: 'May 8, 1945.' "

* * *

I took one last look at "Now It's the Women's Turn," which was foreshortened again into a seeming triangle of close-packed jewels. I did not have to wait for the neighbors and Celeste's schoolmates to arrive before knowing that it was going to be the most popular painting in my collection.

"Jesus, Circe!" I said. "It looks like a million bucks!"

"It really does," she said.

Out went the lights.

37

When we sauntered back to this house through the darkness, she held my hand, and she said I had taken her dancing after all.

"When was that?" I said.

"We're dancing now," she said.

"Oh," I said.

She said again that she couldn't imagine how I or anybody could have made such a big, beautiful painting about something so important.

"I can't believe I did it myself," I said. "Maybe I didn't. Maybe it was done by potato bugs."

She said that she looked at all the Polly Madison

books in Celeste's room one time, and couldn't believe she'd written them.

"Maybe you're a plagiarist," I said.

"That's what I feel like sometimes," she said.

When we reached this house, and although we had not and never would make love, our moods were postcoital. May I say, without seeming boastful, that I had never seen her so *languorous*?

* * *

She surrendered her body, ordinarily so restless, so twitchy and itchy, to a voluptuously cushioned easy chair in the library. Marilee Kemp was in the room, too, in a ghostly way. The bound volume of letters she had written to an Armenian child in California was on the coffee table between me and Mrs. Berman.

I asked Mrs. Berman what she would have thought if the barn had been empty, or if the eight panels had been blanks, or if I had reconstructed "Windsor Blue Number Seventeen."

"If you had really been that empty, which I thought you were," she said, "I guess I would have had to give you an A-plus for sincerity."

* * *

I asked her if she would write. I meant letters to me, but she thought I meant books. "That's all I do—that and dancing," she said. "As long as I keep that up, I keep grief away." All summer long, she had made it easy to forget that she had recently lost a husband who was evidently brilliant and funny and adorable.

"One other thing helps a little bit," she said. "It works for me. It probably wouldn't work for you. That's talking loud and brassy, telling everybody when they're right and wrong, giving orders to everybody: 'Wake up! Cheer up! Get to work!' "

"Twice now I've been a Lazarus," I said. "I died with Terry Kitchen, and Edith brought me back to life again. I died with dear Edith, and Circe Berman brought me back to life again."

"Whoever that is," she said.

*   *   *

We talked some about Gerald Hildreth, the man who would come at eight in the morning to take her and her luggage to the airport in his taxicab. He was a local character about sixty years old. Everybody out this way knows Gerald Hildreth and his taxicab.

"He used to be on the Rescue Squad," I said, "and I think he and my first wife might have had a little fling. He was the one who found Jackson Pollock's body sixty feet from where his car hit the tree. Then, in a few weeks, he was gathering up the pieces of Terry Kitchen's head in a plastic bag. You'd have to say he's played an important part in Art History."

"The last time I rode with him," she said, "he told me his family had been working hard out here for three hundred years, but that all he had to show for it was his taxicab."

"It's a nice taxicab," I said.

"Yes, he keeps it polished on the outside and vacuumed on the inside," she said. "I guess that's how *he* keeps grief away—whatever it is he's got to grieve about."

"Three hundred years," I said.

* * *

We worried about Paul Slazinger. I speculated as to what his helpless soul must have felt like when it realized that his meat had thrown itself down on a hand grenade which was about to go off.

"Why didn't it kill him?" she said.

"Unforgivably sloppy workmanship at the hand grenade factory," I said.

"His meat did that, and *your* meat made the picture in the potato barn," she said.

"Sounds right," I said. "My soul didn't know what kind of picture to paint, but my meat sure did."

She cleared her throat. "Well, then," she said, "isn't it time for your soul, which has been ashamed of your meat for so long, to thank your meat for finally doing something wonderful?"

I thought that over. "That sounds right, too," I said.

"You have to actually *do* it," she said.

"How?" I said.

"Hold your hand in front of your eyes," she said, "and look at those strange and clever animals with love and gratitude, and tell them out loud: 'Thank you, Meat.' "

So I did.

I held my hands in front of my eyes, and I said out loud and with all my heart: 'Thank you, Meat.' "

Oh, happy Meat. Oh, happy Soul. Oh, happy Rabo Karabekian.